SURRENDERED TO THE BERSERKERS

LEE SAVINO

SURRENDERED TO THE BERSERKERS

BY LEE SAVINO

After a thousand years entombed, the Corpse King has broken the witch's binding and risen again. He's raised an army and will rule us all unless we fight and stop him. And I'm the one who holds the key to his defeat.

The witches have tasked me with this mission but they don't trust me. They send two Berserkers to be my guides, my protectors and my guards. Ragnar and Loki are powerful warriors but if they think I'm a naive innocent they can control, they are very much mistaken. I trust them as little as they trust me, and I am on my guard.

What I don't expect is for them to breach my defenses. Bind my worries. Tear down my walls and make me forget my fears. It would be so easy to lose myself to them, but love is a luxury I do not have.

The Berserkers want forever, but I give them one night, because one night is all I have. Tomorrow I face the Corpse King and fight to save everything I hold dear. And in this final battle, I may not survive...

* * *

The Berserker Saga

Berserker Brides

FREE BOOK

Get a secret Berserker book, Bred by the Berserkers (only to
the awesomesauce fans on Lee's email list)
Click here to get started…https://geni.us/BredBerserker

CHAPTER 1

 osalind

THE FOREST WAS thick with towering trees. Thick moss grew between the pines, the bark on the southern sides bearing moss up to the lowest branches. In the deepest thicket, there was no light, just the burnished gold of my hair slipping from its braid, and the eerie glow from the dagger strung on a leather cord around my neck. When I lost my way, I pulled the dagger out of its hiding place and held it aloft, waiting for the moonstone affixed to the pommel to come alive in a blue blaze of eldritch light. The dagger seemed to hum in my hand when I pointed it the correct way. I ignored both the hum of the dagger and its uneasy echo, deep in my breast.

If I could, I'd throw the dagger into the thicket, moonstone and all. But that was not a choice I could make. So I tucked the blade away, and continued on my unwanted quest.

When I'd started walking a day ago, the air had been crisp

with winter, the forest floor covered in snow. The further I walked, the warmer it got. I could not mark the spot where the earth turned from the snowy spring to humid summer. My winter clothes grew heavier with each step. Sweat trickled down my back under the heavy brocade cloak.

You will face many challenges, the witches told me. *The Corpse King loves to pervert the laws of nature and the natural order. He toys with the weather, with the life and death of every creature. But by far his favorite target is the mind.*

I dared not take off the cloak, no matter the growing heat. I would need this cloak at night when the world turned dark. Even if I didn't, I wouldn't set it aside. It was finer than anything I'd ever worn. The hood was fringed with fur. Thick fur lined the boots encasing my feet. As an orphan I'd never been given shoes or nice clothes but it seemed I would be well-dressed as I walked to my death.

My boots left no trace on the carpet of leaves and moss. Even when I stepped too near the stream and sank into the black mud, the water quickly filled in the print. A mere minute after I'd gone, there was no sign that I had passed.

Would the stories tell of me? Rosalind, who carried the world's last weapon into the lair of the enemy? Or would I be forgotten, like a beam of sunlight lingering on a leafy branch, dancing on the surface of a lake—here one moment, gone the next?

I climbed a hill, skirting past thick banks of mountain laurel, pushing past the branches covered with dark green, glossy leaves. My legs ached, and it wasn't even midday. My waterskin was cracked and would hold no more water. I licked my dry lips and soldiered on, keeping close to a stream, trying not to think about where each step was leading me.

We will send help, the witches had told me. But like so many others in my life, they'd lied. And I was alone.

The longer I walked, the more my sense of dread grew. A sound made me pause, but then I realized: there was no sound. The birdsong and the buzz of insects, even the hum of the dagger, had gone quiet.

Then: a slow, shuffling sound. The wind picked up and blew past me, carrying the stench of rot.

I scrambled back from the top of the rise and hid behind an outcropping of boulders, pressing myself to the lichen-clad stone. I must go carefully now. I edged along, keeping the rocks between myself and the creatures below. When I slipped and landed hard on my right ankle, turning it, I did not cry out. My fingernails tore on the rough stone, but I bit my lip and steadied myself. I must make no sound for the enemy to hear.

I leaned on my good leg and hobbled along, ignoring the flashes of pain that went up my right shin. I had more important things to worry about. I limped along until I could peep out of my hiding place.

Below me marched an army of the undead. Grey shapes clad in rags, rotting as they moved. Above the stink, another sickly smell rose—burnt spice and incense, the scent of the herbs they used to cleanse the dead.

I drew back, scrubbing my nose, eyes watering. The longer I lingered, the more I would smell it. And if I stayed too long, it would drive me mad.

The scent came not from herbs or any living thing. It existed only in my mind—the Corpse King's magic made manifest. Not everyone could smell it as I could. And that was another reason I'd been chosen for this quest.

"You have the Corpse King's kiss, my dear." The blind crone passed her thumb over my forehead. *"You see him here. And he is burrowing deeper every day."*

"I do not want this," I said, clenching my fist so I would not rub

my face. "I do not want to have his magic upon me. Remove it. I wish to be ordinary."

"But you were not made to be an ordinary girl. And you know this."

"Why can I not simply remain on the mountain?"

"Do you wish to take a mate?" another witch asked.

"No, but I will if I must." My voice sounded sullen, even to me.

The crone just patted my cheek.

I drew my cloak over my mouth and nose, and pressed a hand to my chest where the dagger lay between my breasts. Under my gown, the moonstone affixed to the dagger's pommel gleamed as it would in the presence of the Corpse King, a tiny spot of blue fire.

I dared not draw the dagger out. It was said the servants of the Corpse King were drawn to the moonstone—first to the moonstone, and then to deliver it to their master. I knew this to be true because I'd once been in the grip of the Corpse King, and felt the same sinister pull to bring the moonstone to him.

Even now, I felt it.

I had to get away from this place.

The sea of draugr—the undead—stretched before me. How was I going to slip past? My fingers fumbled at my pouch. Amid the crumbs of traveling biscuits and scraps of dried meat—my rations that had lasted only a day—were a few weapons the witches had given me.

Use them sparingly, the crone had told me, and only when you see no way forward. I closed my fingers around a rune stone. I had only three of them, and I faced an army of the undead.

Perhaps I would show myself, and they would take me straight to the Corpse King. I could simply walk up to the lurching soldiers and lie down in surrender.

Walk of your own volition into the front gate. This will help deter the Corpse King's hold upon you.

I could not give up so easily. I would have to go around. This would mean leaving the brook, my only source of water. There was no promise I'd find another way around the Corpse King's forces, but I had to try. I could not risk the draugr capturing me.

I crept back down the hill, holding my breath, as if that would help me move more silently. If the undead sensed me here, they would come for me. I had to sneak around them.

But first, a drink from the stream. It was my only source of water, and if I were to leave it, I did not know when I would drink again.

I brushed past the towering ferns, trying to keep my boots out of the muck. Despite my efforts, my left foot got stuck in the black mud. I pulled it free with a sucking sound, staggering a little. A teeth-jarring wave of pain went up my right leg. I'd hurt my ankle more than I originally thought, but there was nothing to do but go on.

I gritted my teeth and limped along a few more steps. Then I halted.

A warrior crouched beside the stream, still as a stump, looking like he'd been there all along. But he hadn't been there a moment before.

I froze, my foot in the air, and stared into his blue eyes. The warrior wore no shirt, only leggings and boots. Leather straps crisscrossed his broad chest. Still crouching, he swiveled towards me with the eerie grace of a man who is not completely human.

"There you are, lass," he said. "I've been looking all over for you."

I licked my lips but could not find my voice. He made no move to come to me, but I took a step back towards the way I came.

The witches had told me they'd send someone to help me. Was this him?

He cocked his head, raising his nose to the breeze. His nostrils flared, and his eyes lit up like torches for the briefest second. "There are draugr over that rise. You're not going that way, are you?"

I rubbed the front of my gown, molding my fingers to the dagger's comforting shape. "It's none of your concern."

The warrior rose to his feet in a fluid, gliding motion, holding my eyes the entire time. While crouching, his bulk had been hidden from me. Now, he reached my height and kept rising, growing into a mountain of muscle and leather and weaponry.

"Ah, lass, but it is my concern." He held out a hand, still moving slowly, as if in water. I jerked back as if he was offering me a snake. "I'm here to take you back."

CHAPTER 2

osalind

"BACK? WHERE?" I asked, stupid for a moment. Then my wits caught up to my mouth. "To Berserker Mountain?" This was not the helper the witches had promised me. This was a Berserker. One of my former captors.

"The Highland pack's land, yes. To safety. Come now." He twitched his fingers in a come-hither motion, as if I was a dog to come when he called. I settled back on my heels so my boots sank further into the mud and leaf mold. "Back to safety. Did you not see the draugr lying in wait over that hill?"

"There's a way around them." I hoped that was true. But I could not hope to outrun or dodge past this warrior. He was huge, a brute, and looked the part. He'd shaved part of his scalp and tied the longer pieces of hair back in braids. His beard was cut short to frame his mouth. The blond stubble hid a hint of a smile, as if I amused him.

"Did the alphas send you?" I asked, stalling for time. "I am known as a troublemaker. I'm surprised they would not just let me go."

"There are too few women for us to lose one. You are all precious to us." His voice deepened to a murmur barely heard above the rippling brook, and when he tilted his head, his eyes flashed bright. Blue one second, gold the next.

My lip curled. "So that is why they care. I am to be a broodmare, like the others."

"Not a mare, no. Not to be ridden in the same way—"

I could not run through him, or past him. So I turned and ran back up the hill, towards the draugr. If I had to choose between running towards the warrior or the evil undead, the Corpse King's troops were the lesser risk.

My breath sawed through my chest as I pelted up the heights, great clumps of fallen leaves and hidden rocks tore away under my feet, threatening my balance. My ankle twinged and shot pains up my leg. But I made it to the flock of boulders where I'd lingered before, scouting my way forward. I was almost past the largest stone when a hard arm caught me around my chest, and a hand clamped over my mouth.

"Got you," the warrior grunted, dragging me back. I fought, thrashing, clawing at his forearm, but it might as well have been an iron band around my middle.

The warrior dragged me back. My legs kicked wildly, the weights in my pouch banging against my thigh, bruising it.

"Be calm," he growled. He was taking me back the wrong way. The quest would never be finished.

Each step west was one I'd have to retrace. My eyes burned, my throat closing. My ankle throbbed.

Damn this warrior. I could not fight him. I'd walked a day and a night, and my food was gone. My stomach was hollow and my limbs were weak, so weak. I could struggle all I wanted and he'd barely notice.

I forced my body to relax. As I stopped struggling, he slowly loosened his hold. A few more steps, and he dropped his hand from my mouth. His scent surrounded me, dry and fresh, with a touch of sweetness, like freshly chopped cedar wood.

"You're making a mistake," I said with calm I did not feel.

His steps didn't falter. "It's not safe for you to be out and about," he murmured in my ear.

"I know that," I snapped. Did he think I was stupid? "I must go on. Our lives depend on it."

We were back by the stream, deeper into the thicket. He set me down, twitching my gown and cloak into place before I found my footing and could push him away.

"Our lives? Do tell." His lips quirked under his beard.

Tell no one of your quest in the open air, lest the Corpse King hear you and learn our plans.

I opened my mouth anyway but the words caught in my throat. An invisible hand strangling me, garbling my ability to speak.

"I can't tell you." I touched my throat, as if my fingers could claw out the words stuck inside. It was no use. The fist around my neck loosened, and I panted for breath.

"Well, then, you'll tell the alphas when we get to the pack lands." Before I could get away, the warrior pulled me down to sit upon a moss-covered log. "Let me see your leg. You were favoring the one."

I would have slapped at his hands, but he tugged my right leg forward, forcing me to grip the crumbling log for balance. While I was busy keeping myself steady, he folded up the hem of my gown and held my calf firm to slide off my boot.

He bowed his head, so close to mine I could make out the light pattern of freckles along his brow.

I sucked in a breath as his fingers traced along the unbroken skin.

He raised his head. "Does that hurt?"

I shook my head and tried again to pull my leg away. "It's just tender."

He didn't release me but his hands were gentle. I bit my lip as he eased my foot in one direction, then the other. My leg was as pale as the underbelly of a mushroom compared to the golden tone of his strong hands.

"There's some stiffness," he murmured. "No sign of swelling."

My breath hissed between my teeth as his touch explored my sore shin. "I landed on it wrong, up by the boulders."

A short nod, and he took out a long strip of leather and bound my ankle. Both of our heads bent together and our breath mingled as he worked. Under his blond scruff, his face was well-shaped. I didn't often stare at a Berserker long enough to admire his looks, but this one had caught my eye before. I remembered him from when I was imprisoned on Berserker Mountain. Even his slightly crooked nose added a harsh masculinity to his looks, making him more handsome.

No. Lusting after a warrior, even one so broad-chested and fine as this one, was not a luxury I could have. He was my captor, nothing more.

"You shouldn't be out here, lass." His voice was mild, but underneath was Damascus steel.

I rubbed my face. I was so tired. "I must continue on," I said. "I cannot tell you why, but it is important."

"All right, lass." His blue eyes seemed sympathetic. "I am here to help you. You don't want to be found by those walking corpses." He shook his head, his large hands binding up my hurt with deft movements. He tucked my dress back down but didn't let me rise. He kept hold of my leg and lifted it, examining my boots. "These are well made. Did a warrior give them to you?"

He was asking if one of his fellow Berserker warriors had wooed me with gifts.

"No." I jerked my foot away and put my back to him. My chest tightened so it was hard to breathe. I was caught. All was lost.

Why hadn't the witches warned the Berserker Alphas of their plans? Now my quest was over before it had truly begun.

A slight tug on my hair made me turn. The warrior had an unruly strand of my long hair between his thumb and forefinger, stroking the silky skein.

"So you've not been courted by any man?" That deep timber to his voice reverberated deep inside me.

"No," I said, and yanked my hair from his grasp. He kept rubbing his thumb and finger together, looking thoughtful.

I forced myself to look away before he saw me admiring the nimbleness of his blunt fingers or his smoothly muscled forearms glinting with gold hair.

He'd asked if a man had courted me. "Why do you care?"

"You are a spaewife, a perfect mate for a Berserker warrior. It is high time you find a mate. Is that why you ran?"

"No." I shut my eyes. "Yes." Perhaps. All winter, I'd lain in the lodge of unmated spaewives, wishing for a way out. And now here it was, but it would lead to my death.

The warrior's large fingers closed around my wrist. Though his fingers were calloused and would be strong as a shackle if I tested him, his grip was gentle.

"It's all right, lass," he said, "I'll return you to the mountain, safe and sound."

The warrior helped me to my feet and pulled me along

after him. I followed, stumbling a little. The bindings on my ankle made it more sturdy, but I was so tired.

Back in the orphanage, my sister used to play with a doll made of corn stalks and straw. I felt as fragile as that hollow figure, made of bits of nothing. One wind would blow me away.

I followed the Berserker without protest. I could not fight him. I would have to find another way to escape.

"What's your name?" I asked, my voice dull as the blade of the dagger hidden on the thong around my neck.

"Ragnar. And you are Rosalind."

* * *

Ragnar

WHEN I FIRST SAW ROSALIND IN the forest, hair gleaming like a vein of gold, skin moon pale, I thought she was a goddess.

She looked tall for a woman, but was not truly of any great height. Her slenderness made her seem taller than she was. Rosalind was a blade of fine steel, tempered in fire, and ready to strike the first man who ventured close.

"You know my name." Her mouth had its usual haughty curve. "What do you know of me?"

"Only what the Alphas told us. You were taken from the abbey the night it was destroyed. You are a spaewife of great beauty." My voice thickened.

She shook her head and looked away, but her cheeks had pinked. She wasn't immune to my interest.

I went on, a pleased note in my tone. "Your sister was rescued from the abbey with you."

Rosalind sniffed but didn't interrupt. I took her arm and

guided her closer to the stream. There I crouched to fill my waterskin.

She looked up and down the bank, studying the black mud.

"What are you looking for?" I asked, handing her the waterskin and prodding it when she hesitated to drink.

"My footprints. They are gone." Her mouth twisted into a mockery of a smile before she lifted the waterskin to her lips.

I held still as a hunter fixed on his prey, watching her throat work as she drank. I'd never seen Rosalind look happy —truly happy, rested and at peace. She'd gone about Berserker Mountain with a fixed expression. Some would call it haughty. I called it haunted.

"Something happened to you," I mused. "Some terrible thing."

She scoffed and wiped her mouth. "You could say that."

It came to me. "I remember. On the way, you were lost, caught in the grip of the Corpse King. A storm of his making. His magic swirled all around you, creating a fog. The warriors defended you, and were attacked by the undead soldiers. They fought free and rescued all the spaewives they brought with them but you were lost for days, wandering in the fog."

She handed back the waterskin and I crouched to refill it. While she thought I wasn't looking, she smoothed the front of her gown. There was a shape of a small dagger outlined beneath it. Its blade must be dull enough for it to rest between her breasts. If so, it wouldn't do much good against an attacker. Not that any weapons would deter a Berserker.

"I remember," Rosalind whispered. She raised a trembling hand to her throat, but her voice held steady. "I held my sister's hand, and prayed I could keep her safe."

She had a sister, a young one, back on Berserker Mountain. I tried to recall the name. "Aspen," I said, and bright rage flooded Rosalind's face, washing her fear away.

"Aspen is an innocent. And you dragged us from the only home we'd known." Her small fists clenched at her sides. Her body trembled with the force of her anger—and fatigue, and hunger. She'd been too long in these woods, alone, with no one to care for her. I'd found her just in time.

"We rescued you—"

"You put us in danger. In the Corpse King's path—"

"He was coming for you anyway. You were easy prey in that abbey."

Only a few inches separated us as she glared up at me from her slight height. Facing off with a warrior nearly thrice her size, with no hesitation or self-preservation.

Oh, there was fear in her scent, it had a bitter edge. But she was not afraid of me.

"You warriors took us in the night. Scared us half to death. And then on the way to Berserker Mountain, in the middle of the forest and despite the warriors surrounding us —the ones who should've made us safe—we were attacked."

"That was a tragedy," I admitted. "It should not have happened. I had packmates who died that night." In the dark and confusion, the Corpse King had used his powers to make several of the Berserkers go mad. Several were lost to the beast, and had to be cut down. "It was a horrible time. I wish you had not gone through it. We failed you, lass, and for that, I apologize."

Her lips parted, but she said nothing more. She was speechless, her cheeks flooded with color. Still holding onto her anger but silent, as if my apology had caught her off guard.

"But..." I rallied. "It ended well for you and the rest of the spaewives. You were found and brought to Berserker Mountain—"

"You imprisoned us!"

"And kept you in all comfort."

"Comfort," she spat. This woman would argue with a rock.

"Aye, Rosalind. Comfort. A warm lodge to live in. A dry place to lay your head. Meat and mead and anything your heart desired."

"Except freedom."

I wanted to shake her. "We rescued you."

"You thought you rescued us," she said, the anger dropping from her voice, leaving only a despair that made me ache. "But we were not safe."

"The Corpse King could not reach you on Berserker Mountain."

She dragged a hand over her brow. "His reach was further than you knew."

The bitterness in her scent had a spiced tinge to it. Frankincense and clove—the scent of grave clothes. The scent of the Corpse King's magic clung to Rosalind. The beast inside me roared. Something was wrong.

* * *

ROSALIND

I SPUN ON MY FOOT, putting my back to the warrior as I rubbed the front of my gown. Would that I were a man as big and strong as he. Would that the dagger was a giant sword that could lop his head from his oversized shoulders. That would wipe the smug grin off his stupidly handsome face.

"What do you mean?" His voice thickened into a growl. He sounded like he cared, and something inside me ached, wishing that were true.

I held onto my anger. It was my only shield between me and despair. How dare he speak of the Berserkers' plunder of the abbey as if it was a rescue? I remembered those days of wandering, my sister's hands small and cold in mine. Her trusting innocence resting like a boulder in my breast.

The warriors had dragged us from the only home we'd known. They thought they'd rescued us from the Corpse King, but his reach was longer than they knew. All winter, he'd spoken to me. He came to me in dreams, in visions, and ghostly whispers that echoed in my head until it ached. But this was a secret that no one knew, not even the witches.

I couldn't tell anyone. Especially not this Berserker.

He was at my back, his heat seeping into me, warming my chilled bones. "Tell me, Rosalind."

"It is not your concern."

"But it is. You're in my care now, lass. I'll keep you fed and watered, and deliver you to safety."

I sighed and rubbed the back of my neck, turning back. "Do what you must." I would do my best to thwart him.

Ragnar tipped up the waterskin and drank deeply. A few water droplets clung to his beard. There was no denying it: this Berserker was particularly handsome. And he knew it.

Perhaps I could use his vanity, turn it to my purposes. Like most men who thought me beautiful, he would never guess my looks were a weapon I wielded to my advantage. He'd have no idea how I used my beauty to blind him, until it was too late.

"Do you wish for a mate?" I asked quietly, toying with my hair. Its golden color was not as bright and sunny as my sister's but still drew the men's eyes like a torch. I knew without looking that Ragnar was watching me.

"Most of the pack does." He squatted to fill the waterskin once more. "A favored few have found their mates but I must prove myself first. Fortunately, with the Corpse King rising against us, there will be many battles."

Of course a Berserker would be pleased about the prospect of more battles. *Brute.*

"Do you have a warrior brother?"

"All my fellow warriors are brothers." He shrugged.

"Doesn't the bond grow between two warriors to help keep the Berserker madness at bay?" I knew the answer to my question. I'd learned much over the winter, during my time spent on Berserker mountain.

"It can help," he answered shortly.

"I heard it said each warrior stabilizes the other." I smoothed the lock of my hair and wrinkled my brow. "Does it worry you? That the madness that besets the Berserkers will fall more quickly upon you?"

I knew by the way he looked away from me, peering into the forest shadows with his jaw set like stone, that it did.

"Come," he said more gruffly. "We must not tarry. I wish to be back by dawn." He held out his hand.

I'd traveled most of two days and a night. It seemed he'd return me in half that time.

"I am tired," I complained softly. Searching for sympathy.

"You should've thought of that before you ran." He didn't wait for me to take his hand, he leaned and grabbed mine and tugged me along. I gritted my teeth at his quickened pace.

"Will we walk all night?"

"If we have to."

I huffed and let him half lead, half drag me deeper into the forest. At least my ankle no longer hurt. Not that I'd thank him for his help.

"Are you the only warrior they sent after me?"

"Does it matter?" he asked without turning. "I am the one who caught you."

I caught the triumphant note in his voice. If I could pick at it, dig a little deeper, I might draw blood. "You're proud of that."

No answer. He held up a branch so I might duck under it.

I tried again. "You think the Alphas will give you a reward if you complete your task well."

"The Alphas decreed the remaining spaewives may choose their mates."

"But if you were to prove yourself in some extravagant service, some bravery, they might allow you to choose for yourself." I made my voice soft and sultry, smooth as silk gliding over skin.

He ignored me. When he paused for a moment to sniff the wind, I let my hand hover at his back, an inch above the tanned plane of muscle. "But there's no need to wait. You could have your reward right here, right now." I couldn't keep the tremor out of my voice. I didn't know whom I'd be more annoyed with—him, if he fell for my blatant seduction, or myself, for secretly wanting him to.

He kept his face pointed to the sky, his jaw clenching. "What game are you playing?"

I withdrew my hand. "No game," I lied. It was a simple plan: seduce him. Distract him from his quest. If he fell under my thrall, I could convince him to let me go, or at least stall him until I could slip away.

His head swiveled to skewer me with an icy gaze. "I know when you lie to me."

I froze like a rabbit seen by the hunter. By the wolf. My pulse sped up but I forced myself to answer. My voice was breathless. "Perhaps I like games."

He grunted and took my hand, pulling me along again. "You would not like the game I want to play." His cheek curved under his beard. He was laughing at me. Laughing!

I snatched my hand from his grip. I couldn't stop my rush

of sharp words. "Perhaps the Alphas won't reward you with a mate. Or perhaps they will, but it won't be me. I will tell them I wish to take a mate, and I'll make my choice, but it will be anyone *but* you. You'll have to watch while I'm given to another."

A growl ripped from his chest. I was winning.

"I know you noticed me back on Berserker Mountain," I purred. "I know I'm the one you want. That's why you worked so hard to track me before the rest. But you will never have me—"

Ragnar's hand whipped out and closed over my arm. He swung me around and forced my feet to retreat until my back was against the wide trunk of an oak.

His huge chest heaved as he whispered, "Be careful, Rosalind. I pledged to save you. But I am a Berserker. And I have little patience. You'd do well to obey."

Pressed up against the tree, my head tilted to look up at him, I felt the heavy length of his arousal, big as a club against my leg.

"You wouldn't dare—"

He leaned in so close, my breasts brushed his bare chest. Even through my gown, the hard muscle abraded my sensitive nipples. Heat shot through me, blooming on my cheeks.

"Try me." His whisper tickled my ear. "I'd love to make you behave." The fine hairs on the back of my neck rose, but the rest of my body reacted like he'd promised me pleasure, not punishment. My belly tightened against the rush of nectar between my legs.

I swallowed my snarling response and nodded.

He held me fast for a few more heartbeats, then stepped back and took my hand again.

"Come. We have a long way to go."

* * *

I HELD my peace the rest of the day. I looked for opportunities to escape, but Ragnar kept hold of me the whole time. Better to bide my time and reserve my strength for the right moment. But as the day gave way to darkness and the moon rose, I let my head bow. I was the picture of cowed obedience —too tired to show strength. It looked as if Ragnar would make us walk all night.

Then, when we entered a green space between the pines, he stopped and slung his pack at the foot of a tree. "Let us stop here for shelter."

Finally. I raised my head. Night had settled upon us but the moon was almost full, casting enough light for me to see.

I headed for a tree to relieve my needs. Ragnar stopped me with a hard hand on my arm.

"I need a moment," I snapped.

"So you can run away?"

I raised my chin. "I require privacy. I will not run. I promise."

"I'll hold you to your promise." He released me "If you run, Rosalind, I will hunt you. And you will not like the consequences."

I held his eyes until I'd stepped behind a tree. I crouched for a moment, making sure I was hidden.

Back in the glade, Ragnar was making use of his axe to chop wood and build a fire.

Still bent in half, I slipped between the ferns, and ran.

I held my skirts up around my knees and cursed my heavy pouch. Even the dagger seemed heavier between my breasts.

My legs burned from the efforts of the day and my travels the day before but new energy shot through my body as I ran. My ankle protested my pace, but I could put my weight on it without pain. Ragnar had taken such care to bind my ankle, and now his care would help me escape him.

Leaves and branches whipped my face and hands. I crashed through the thick bushes. Dark, glossy leaves whipped my face. A branch sliced my cheek. It didn't matter. I would run through a thorny briar patch if I had to. Anything to get away from the roaring monster who was chasing me. My rushing blood and heartbeat roared like a storm in my ears. *Don't look back.*

My legs betrayed me, and I stumbled. I caught myself once before overbalancing and crashing to the forest floor. My hands scrabbled in the moss, ripping up chunks of earth as I hoisted myself up.

I staggered to my feet. The monster was almost upon me. I shied to the left, pressing myself against a trunk to catch my breath. Perhaps I could hide. Perhaps the monster's senses would be confused, and I could dart away when it was not looking. Perhaps—

A beastly claw closed around my upper arm. Ragnar tugged me from my hiding place. I got a quick glimpse of the terrifying face—the wolf's snout, the fur sprouting black in tufts over his body. Half man, half beast, a sleek shape melded from both forms. Huge. Monstrous. Cloaked in black fur and darkness.

I shut my eyes.

The beast wrenched me onto my back. I lay vulnerable, palms up at my sides, as the monster drew over me. If the beast ripped out my throat, I would be powerless to stop it.

Hot breath hit my face. The monster's weight pinned me down as he explored me, sniffing up my neck then down to my chest, where he drew back sharply. I couldn't help it. I opened my eyes. The dangerous beast hovering over me woke every elemental fear in me. His fur brushed my arms.

I licked my lips. "Ragnar," I whispered, my voice a hoarse rasp. Maybe I could call the man back to himself.

"Quiet," the monster muttered in Ragnar's voice. Maybe

he hadn't lost himself, yet. Golden eyes shone, bright torches in the night. The monstrous bulk of Ragnar was bigger than the man. Muscles bunched in his forearms, his elbows ending in tufts of black fur. The forearms were those of a wolf. A beast. The paws were as big as my head. The claws— monstrous black crescents—curved like skinning knives.

My teeth clacked together. Deep inside, this monster was a Berserker, and he desired me. Even now, his cock prodded my belly.

"Ragnar. Please."

His body stiffened, arched backwards. The beast raised his head to the dark sky, and let out a half roar that ended in two melancholy notes. A long, chilling howl.

Last winter, I had lain at night in my bed and listened to the Berserkers howling. Celebrating the camaraderie of the pack. Mourning the loneliness of their existence. Hoping for a Berserker bride.

Now, the sound vibrated through me. I longed to scrub my arms free of goosebumps. But I dared not move.

"Rosalind," the beast murmured, and his fur was receding. My fingers twitched. If I raised my hand, I could stroke the features and feel them emerge from the beast-like form. Feel the face taking shape—the wolf's snout receding, giving way to the long, human nose. Ragnar's nose, broken at the top in some ancient brawl. The proud brow, the broad cheeks covered in stubble. For some reason, his beard looked shorter, as if it had been shorn off only a few days ago.

Finally, the bright blue eyes appeared, along with the half-shaved head and braids.

I did touch him then, tracing his brows, running my fingers over the shape of his mouth.

"You came back to me," I said.

Ragnar was braced over me, his strong arms planted on either side of my body. His whole body shuddered.

"Yes. But it was close." And he lowered his head, his beard scraping my face as he slanted his mouth across mine, kissing me with all the savagery of a monster. I tensed, and then something broke through my chest. I embraced him, my arms twining around his shoulders as I kissed him back with all the passion in me. Our tongues tangled and fought. And my body rose up to meet him. My core ached. If I could only press against him—

He wrenched away, leaving me shivering on the ground. He rose, still somehow clad in breeches, and the leather straps crisscrossing his chest. One was broken from the Change—the muscular bulk of the beast had strained and snapped it. He ripped it off and flung it away. Then he reached down and hoisted me up, tossing me over his shoulder. His hand smacked my rump and I let out a squawk.

"That's for lying."

"Ragnar!" I kicked but couldn't get free. He banded an arm around my legs and smacked my upturned bottom again. "Be still. Remember what I told you? You ran, now you face the consequences."

 osalind

RAGNAR TOSSED me down next to a pile of sticks and brush he'd gathered, and went back to building a fire. Calmly, as if nothing had happened.

I shifted to my hip. My rump still stung from his swats. My backside probably bore the imprint of his hand. I crossed my legs and started pulling leaves and twigs out of my hair. "I had to try."

"Why?" he growled. "There's nothing out there for you. Only danger. Here is safety. Why would you run?"

"To be free," I burst out.

His shadow fell over me but he only set the waterskin down beside me. "What is freedom if it kills you?"

"Spoken like someone who's never known a cage," I snapped back, shifting on my sore rear.

"We all live in cages. Big and small, mostly of our own making. There's no power so infinite that you can escape everything you hate."

"I can try," I muttered, digging my heels into the dirt. "At least I'll escape you."

"There is no escaping me."

He got the fire going and pulled out a leaf-wrapped packet of dried meat. When he held a strip of jerky in front of my face, I set my jaw, ignoring my gurgling stomach.

"No." I wrapped my arms around my knees.

"Yes, Rosalind. You must eat to keep up your strength. Especially if you plan to keep fighting me."

He was right. I swiped the meat from his hand and chewed sullenly.

The fire crackled between us. He gave me more meat, as I needed, and we passed the waterskin between us.

"It will not be so bad, back on the mountain," he said softly. "You will be safe."

"Have you ever been a captive?"

"Not in the same way."

He got up to chop more wood to replenish the dimming fire. In his absence, I considered what he meant. The Berserker madness was a sort of captivity. What would it be like to live for so many years, so powerful, never knowing when your own mind would betray you?

"I'm sorry," I said when he returned. "It was cruel to mention the madness."

"You're forgiven." He finished stacking the logs on the blaze and dusted off his hands. "Are you finished eating?"

I took one more pull from the waterskin and wiped my mouth. "Yes, thank you."

"Good girl." He shrugged out of the leather straps, laying them aside along with his sheathed weapons. "Now," he said. "There's the matter of your punishment."

My last mouthful of meat turned to sand. "Punishment?"

"You disobeyed me."

I swallowed. "I never promised I would obey."

"You will submit to my word as law until we reach our home."

"The mountain is not my home," I snapped. "I have no home."

That gave him pause. "Still." He patted his knee.

I raised my chin. "If you think I'm going to crawl to you for my punishment—"

"You need not crawl," he purred, "unless you wish it."

His arm snapped forward and grabbed my wrist. In a swift move, he'd hauled me over his lap.

I kicked as he tossed up my skirts, but his arm pinned me and I couldn't escape. The air hit my bare skin and I went still. My lower half was totally exposed, vulnerable.

"Is this wise?" I asked, raising my head. I was face down, my hair hanging into the dirt. He took care to gather the blonde strands back, and fussed with it as I had before, picking out the leaves as I lay with my bare bottom in the wind.

"Is what wise?" His voice rasped like a knife scraping against a whetstone.

"Is it wise to toy with me this way?" I kept my voice even. "If the beast is so close to the surface…"

"It pleases the beast to punish you." His hand settled on my bare rear and I jumped. "Now be still."

I tensed as he caressed my bottom. Ragnar's knees and the muscles of his thigh were hard under my torso, but his hand was gentle as he rubbed my sensitive skin.

"Will you get it over with?" I made my voice sharp but it came out breathy.

He chuckled. "You test a man's mettle." He stroked a finger lower, between my legs. "Your cunny, unlike your mouth, does not lie. You like this, Rosalind."

Heat curled through me at his touch. "I do not like this," I denied. "I do not want this. You are in danger of turning into the beast—"

"You should have thought of that before you ran." Then his hand crashed down on my bare flesh. A warning strike, more sound than sting. I yelped and wriggled. His opposite hand settled into the small of my back to steady me. "These are consequences," he said. "Do not run from me again."

"And if I do?" I could not stop myself from challenging.

"If you do, I will teach you this lesson again." And his hand crashed down, spanking me soundly, his palm connecting with each buttock in turn.

I bit my lip so I would not cry out. I would not give him the satisfaction. Then his fingers snuck between my legs, and I gasped.

"Ragnar!" I thrashed a little, and he smacked my bottom hard enough to make me blink.

"Be still," he ordered. "I am in control. This is your punishment."

His hand cupped the heated flush of my bottom. It throbbed, the flesh molten. Would that it would sear his palm!

"It would please me, Rosalind," he purred, "if you run again." And he slipped two fingers between my legs to rest atop my folds. I almost cried out because it would only take a few strokes and I would find relief. Desire pooled in my belly.

My bottom twitched but I dared not move.

"This is unfair," I ground out. I was on a quest not of my own making. I'd been promised help and Ragnar was the opposite, sent by the Alphas out of a misunderstanding.

"Life's not fair, little runaway." His fingers moved very slightly, tapping my labia. If only he would delve deeper into the folds and find the slippery nubbin between them.

I had never felt desire like this blazing into every corner

27

of my body. My sex was dripping. The scent of it flared around me. Ragnar inhaled, and a rumble rose from deep in his chest. The sound settled into my bones.

A curious sensation came over me, and I went limp over his lap. A sort of surrender.

Who knew that surrender would be so sweet?

"That's it," he murmured, a mere whisper.

He moved his fingers, touching me deftly. He stroked my folds, finding my soaked entrance and exploring the edge of it.

"Rosalind." His hand moved away and I heard him lick his fingers. Under my belly, his cock was rigid. "Rosalind, I never knew…" His fingers went to my folds again, teasing, touching, dancing lightly around my pleasure spots. Pushing me to the brink. If I could wriggle my hips, I would go over but when I moved, Ragnar took his hand away from the delicious doings between my legs to smack my bottom again.

"Who's in control?"

I hung my head. "You are."

"And who will you obey?"

"You." My voice cracked. *For now.*

As if he could hear my defiance, Ragnar commanded, "Say it again."

"I will obey you," I shouted, my voice tense, defiant.

"That's right. And if you run, you will be punished. But if you obey…"

I held my breath. His palm slid over my chastised bottom and delved between my legs.

"Eventually, you will find reward." His fingers nudged at a sweet spot deep in my folds. Pleasure flared in a faint golden arc through my body, promising a richer sensation to come.

But he withdrew his fingers.

"Not tonight. You have not earned it."

I grit my teeth so I wouldn't cry out. There was a storm

rising in me, a gale of need and savage longing. And frustration. I wanted to howl.

He drew me up, straightening my clothes. I clenched my fists to keep from slapping him away. He brushed my face where a tear had escaped to slide down my cheek. "Are you well?"

"I'm fine," I snapped. He let me stalk to my side of the campfire. "I hate you."

"You didn't like me before. I've suffered no loss." He licked his fingers again, then banked the fire and laid out a thick cloak. "Come." He held out a hand to me.

I glowered at him.

"Rosalind. If I had my way, I would've journeyed all night, carrying you when you could go no further. Is that what you wish to do?"

"No."

"Then come." His beard hid the amused tilt to his mouth.

My feet dragged the whole way. "I don't wish to lie next to you."

"Consider it part of your punishment." He tugged me down and took both my wrists to wrap a leather thong around them, tight.

I ground my teeth, and his lips quirked enough to flash a white fang.

"Punishment, little runaway."

He rolled me to my side and tucked me against him. I lay curled in the strong shelter of his powerful body. One large hand reached around to check the ties around my wrist, then slid to cup my hip. My backside prickled with the memory of his hard palm. I could fight and try to wrestle him away on principle, but it would do nothing. His muscular legs were like tree trucks compared to mine.

"Sleep, now," he ordered. "We will travel home in the morning."

"It's not my home. I've never had a home." Only cages, some larger, some smaller, but none big enough to allow me to breathe.

His voice, when it came, was far away. "I'm sorry, little runaway." But I was too far gone in the grip of sleep to answer.

* * *

I WOULD NOT HAVE SUCCUMBED to sleep so easily if I had known what was waiting for me. In my dream, I lay blanketed in a pool of mist. Huge pines towered over me. Beyond them, dark shapes ran through the forest—Berserkers fighting unseen enemies.

A ghostly form rose up before me, the mist blowing away until only a hooded shape remained. A cloaked man, tall and thin, with bone-white hands. The fingers stretched towards me. *Rosalind...*

In the distance, a raven cawed. *Follow the Raven*, the crone's voice prompted. But I couldn't see or hear where the bird had gone, much less follow. My legs were stuck as if the thick mist was a mire.

The cloaked man snapped his long fingers, and we were standing on a cliff. Below us, stretching for miles like a silvery sea, was an army in shining armor. Rank upon rank of helmeted troops, standing in eerie silence. Beyond them rose a castle made of obsidian stone. Its gate was tall as a mountain, and its turrets disappeared into the clouds.

All of this will be yours, the cloaked man told me. *Make your choice.*

The wind whipped at my skirts. "Take off your hood," I ordered with frozen lips.

The man raised his pale hands and pushed back his hood.

The face he revealed was a skeleton. I opened my mouth to scream—

A low rumble jolted me awake. I lay on my side, Ragnar at my back. The moon hung high above us, a bright coin, almost perfectly round.

My body was enveloped in heat. My neck was bent, and fur brushed my bare skin.

"Ragnar?" I slurred, disoriented.

A paw slid into my line of sight, reaching for me. Moonlight glinted on the long claws. I flinched away but the monster caught my shoulder and rolled me onto my back.

"Rosalind." Ragnar's voice was swallowed in the guttural growl of a beast. His dark bulk loomed over me, covered in fur.

My body stiffened, my heart booming out of my chest.

This was not Ragnar. This was a Berserker out of control. The beast was upon him.

"Rosalind," he rasped.

"What happened?" I whispered. Perhaps there was enough of Ragnar to answer. Perhaps I could keep him talking, keep him reasoning with me…

"Your presence wakes the beast."

I was going to die. I started to struggle, but my hands were bound.

"No, be still. I will not hurt you." The dark shape of his head lowered. Black fur, glinting teeth shining like daggers.

I closed my eyes.

The beast who was also Ragnar nuzzled my neck. "The beast is hungry for you." Something brushed my shoulder—a tooth? A claw? "Be still," Ragnar muttered, his breath hot on my face. "Be very still."

The monster braced over me, huge, fur-covered arms on either side of my head. Heat shimmered between us. Sweat trickled down my temple, and lower down... need flared between my legs.

He lowered his head and scented along my jawline. So close, so hot. He still smelled like Ragnar, like fresh cedar shavings. A calming scent.

Something changed between us—energy shifting. Like a crackle of lightning, unseen but enough to raise the hair on my arms. Fear tipping into anticipation.

I shifted my hips very slightly. For some unknown reason, my breasts were swollen, aching.

The monster nudged further down my body. One lunge, and its teeth could be at my throat, ripping out my heart. Fur brushed the sensitive skin over my collarbone. The beast's head hovered over my chest, nuzzling there. When it nosed the dagger, the moonstone flared and the creature flinched as if it had bitten him.

I tensed. The return of fear washed all my desire away. "Ragnar," I whispered. "Come back to me."

"I'm here," he answered in a slow, lazy voice. He'd reared back, his dark shape blocking out the sky. I lay in his shadow, the only light the glow of his eyes.

I licked my lips. "What do I do?"

"Do not fight. Do not run. Do not fear."

I swallowed. Each breath I took felt heavy going down. "I cannot help how I feel," I said. I always spoke when I was afraid, as if my words would ward off my terror.

"You have no need to fear me." He sounded drunk. Moonlight flooded my eyes as he lurched off me. The weight of the beast left me, but the heat remained. He settled behind me again.

I lay next to the mountain of fur and fangs, wondering when the beast would transform and give me back Ragnar. Afraid to check behind me to see.

When he spoke again, his voice was clear. "Peace, Rosalind. You please the beast."

My limbs relaxed. I sprawled on my side. When Ragnar's furred arm came around to grip me tighter to him, I was too tired to care. The bulk beside me was warm as a banked fire, and soft as a wolf's pelt.

It shouldn't have soothed me but it did.

This monster was the strongest thing in the forest tonight. There was no need to be afraid. Sheltered in the beast's hold, I was safe from everything.

Even my darkest dreams.

 osalind

I WOKE when dawn's light hit my face. Ragnar was already up and spreading leaves over the charred remains of last night's fire, eliminating all traces of our presence. He was fully a man, though his hair seemed longer and his shoulders looked broader.

I stepped behind a tree to see to my needs and freshen up, doing the best I could with the thong still tying my hands together. I knelt by a stream to splash my face, and managed to loosely braid my hair. Ragnar held the waterskin for me to drink from, and gave me a hardtack biscuit to nibble.

We said nothing of what had happened the night before.

When it was time to go, he stopped and checked the bindings around my wrists, taking the end of one strap in his hand.

My irritation boiled over. There was no sign of Ragnar

the beast. No fear to curb my tongue. "When will you untie me?"

"When you can be trusted." He grasped the end and led me away on my short leash.

I ground my teeth. But what could I do? I marched behind him. It was time to test his patience.

"What a beautiful morning," I murmured, honey dripping from my tone.

Ragnar snapped his head to face me, his brow furrowed. I gave him a small, serene smile, mimicking a statue I'd once seen of the Madonna. As I walked beside him, I swished my hips. "But I fear it will be a hot one. The sweat is trickling down my back. Would that I could shed this dress."

"And walk nude?" He sounded intrigued.

I lifted a shoulder in a half shrug. "It would be cooler, no?"

"Enough talk. We cannot dawdle." He quickened the pace and I smiled at his back. I had found a way to annoy him.

"The bluebells are very fine in this place." I spoke about whatever popped into my head. Mostly talk about the weather, the flowers, the bright sun, the state of my hair.

"I swear upon my father's grave, I've never heard anybody chatter like you," he grumbled.

"This is what you chose," I said. "You, of all the Berserkers, chose to hunt me."

"Oh, many were sent to hunt. I was simply the most successful. I traveled far with no food in my belly. No stopping. It was as if your scent was in my lungs." He grasped a handful of my hair and brought it to his nose, inhaling. His eyes flashed gold.

My legs grew weak, my blood turning to simmering honey. "I hope it was worth it." I made my voice tart.

He released my hair and tipped back his head to scent the

air. The aroma of my wet sex was thick around us. His cheek curved into a grin. "It was."

I glared daggers into his back. My nails dug into the bonds, but I couldn't work my wrists free.

If I could not escape, I would make him pay. He would be as miserable as I, the whole way back.

"Do all Berserkers carry an axe and a sword?" I asked as we walked on.

"Warriors carry what they will."

"Are you a lesser warrior, then, to carry two weapons?" I kept my voice light, my eyes wide and innocent. "I would think most would make do with one."

Ragnar stopped short, tugging me to a halt. I ground my teeth at being so leashed. His face was impassive, not a hint of annoyance, but it was there, lurking under the surface.

"In truth, it takes double skill to carry double the weapons. Each one has a different weight and heft, and requires a different technique." He pulled me onward. "Of course, Berserkers have no need of weapons when we have the beast. Teeth and claws."

"Right." I hid my shudder.

"Does the beast frighten you?"

"I am sane, so yes, it frightens me," I snapped. "Only a fool or a madman would walk bravely into danger."

"And yet you were walking toward the Corpse King's lands," Ragnar mused, taking the lead to guide me out of a field and into a thicker forest. "The greatest danger our world has known."

I had no response to that. I was too busy trying to keep my skirts from catching on the raspberry briars that grew across our path. No matter how I twisted, with my wrists bound, I could do nothing but hiss at the thorns that tore my hem.

And then I was up in the air, feet swinging over the

ground, scooped into Ragnar's arms. He hoisted me effort-lessly against him, as if I was naught but a bit of dandelion fluff, and strode into the thicket. He leapt and sailed over the brambles, jumping from tussock to tussock. His boots crunched the thorns underfoot without ever getting torn. I held my breath. Being so close, the scent of his sweat and leather rolled over me like a haze. His muscles flexed. I fought the urge to hold tight—and lost. Again, there was a hint of a smile hidden in the corner of his beard.

"Well, Rosalind?" he asked. His eyes were a discon-certing blue in his weathered face. "Will you tell me why you were on the run? Heading towards the Corpse King, no less?"

I couldn't tell him. Not with the thrice-damned silencing spell upon me.

"Perhaps I preferred the danger to being the captive of the Berserkers," I said as snippily as I could. I turned my face away from his intense stare. Up close, Ragnar could see all my secrets. I had a feeling he was not fooled by my haughty veneer.

"You shun safety so easily?"

"I have known safety—in the orphanage," I sneered. "Per-haps I prefer freedom to safety."

He carried me a few more paces before murmuring, "I could build you a home. If you'd let me."

I bit back a verbal attack. Ragnar held me easily, his arms locked around me. His face was too close, his eyes too blue.

Perhaps it was cowardice that made me hold my tongue. Perhaps fear of enraging the beast.

He strode from the forest into another field. There were buildings in the distance—a farm. But Ragnar kept to the edges of the fallow field, near the forest.

"Will you put me down?" I asked. He swung me down without comment. I tucked my cloak around me more closely, shivering not so much from the cool morning air, but the loss of Ragnar's warmth.

He kept a hand on my elbow, continuing to steer me.

"What would you do, if you were not kept by the Berserkers?" he asked.

I rolled my eyes. "Be free."

"Would you want a man?"

"No."

"None?" Ragnar's blue eyes twinkled. "Not even a rich one?"

"None," I repeated.

He guided me to walk along a rock wall, built to hem in cattle. "So you'd be a nun?"

"No," I snapped and sucked in a breath. "No," I said more calmly. Nuns were crones, shriveled and cruel, with no love in them. At least, that was my experience with them, back at the abbey.

"Then where would you live?"

"By the sea. Somewhere I could see for miles and miles."

I watched closely to see if his expression held rancor, but he only looked thoughtful. "Would you have a house? A hut? A castle?"

A castle built of thick stone no army can penetrate. I bit back that first response which came, I feared, from a darker part of me. For a moment, I remembered my dream with the hooded man, the castle, and the army waiting for its commands. Then I pushed it away.

"Something like this would suffice." I gestured to the farm in the distance, the buildings with stone walls and thatched roofs. Someone had planted a riot of flowers up against the fence. "I'd own my own land. I'd garden, and plant crops." *Or have servants to do so.*

"And that is truly what you want?"

"Yes." I looked down my nose at him, which took some

talent, since he was a head taller than I. "I suppose you always wanted a mate? Some little woman to do your bidding?"

He was silent, guiding me back into the forest. "No," he said finally, surprising me. "I never thought I'd have a mate."

"Not even to appease the beast?" I was breaking the rules, speaking of the unspeakable. As if mentioning the beast would conjure it.

"I did not think I would survive long enough to find one."

For some reason, this hurt my heart. I should not care about this big, brooding Berserker, but my emotions knew no reason.

"And if you did?" I asked. I wasn't teasing him, not now. "If you found the one who could soothe the beast, would you want a mate?"

"It's not to be."

"How can you say that? Will the Alphas not grant you a mate?"

"Does it matter, Rosalind?" Under his beard, the corner of his mouth quirked up.

"Why should all the Berserkers get mates, and not you? It's not fair. "

He chuckled. "I didn't realize it mattered so much to you."

I wanted to insist it didn't, but he would know I was lying. "Indulge me. If you were able to take a mate, where would you live?"

"Wherever she wanted."

"You wouldn't want a huge lodge to call home?"

He pushed aside a branch that was in my way. "I would not need a lodge to call home if I had a mate. Wherever she was, that would be my home."

Longing struck me like an arrow from a bow. I glided past him, turning my head to hide my expression.

"A simple dream," I said with all the mocking I could muster—when I could speak again.

"So is yours." Ragnar bent close to me. His whispered growl made the hair on the back of my neck stand up. "But I feel you have not given me the full tale of what you truly want. Tell me, Rosalind... what do you dream of?"

"Power." The word burst from me. "I want power, such that no one can stand against me." *So no one will hurt me again.*

Ragnar tugged on my leash and I whirled to face him, my lungs working like bellows. He looked me slowly up and down. My fists clenched at my sides.

"I wanted power too. Once. Long ago." He studied the leather end in his hand. "Be careful, Rosalind, what you wish for."

Easy for you to say, I almost spat to the man who held my leash.

He turned to lead me on, and I followed, taking care to keep the leash slack. We made our way back into the forest, and when the hut and the flower garden disappeared from sight, I wasn't sorry.

Each step we took sent me back to captivity. I'd been captive all my life, one way or another. There was no escape.

But at least I wasn't headed to my death. I could tell the witches I had failed. The thought made me stumble. Ragnar caught me, and walked more slowly. My eyes stung as sweat rolled into them. I used my forearm to wipe it away.

As we followed the stream's path out of the forest, the sun was high in the sky. Ragnar halted, holding my leash fast. He raised his head to sniff the wind.

"What is it?" I kept my voice low.

"A stench on the wind." His eyes flared bright as torches. Slowly, he swiveled his head. "Draugr."

The undead warriors of the Corpse King.

"Come." He broke into a trot. I tried to keep up, my pouch swinging heavily and hitting my thigh. Ragnar slowed his pace enough so I could slog along beside him the best I could, but impatience showed through the tight lines of his face.

He guided me across the stream and into a grove of pine. Barely any light trickled down to us as we made our way over a rust-colored carpet. The end of the grove was abrupt. Axes had chopped down trees—the stumps were worn with age. Ahead lay the farm of stone huts, just like the ones we'd passed before.

"Is this the way?" I asked. The farm looked so familiar. "Ragnar—"

"We're going in circles. Something is wrong." He shook his head as if flies were pestering him. "I thought…" He slowed, stepping in one direction, then another. "The Corpse King playing tricks," he muttered.

He swiveled to me, dropping the leash.

"Here." He undid the bindings around my wrists and pocketed the leather tie. His big hands checked over my wrists, his thumbs rubbing the red marks the thong had left on my skin.

Warmth grew in my belly at his touch—my body responding, even though now was not the time.

"Stay close," Ragnar ordered, releasing me. I did as he asked. He trusted me enough to remain untied. I would obey —for now.

I squinted at him. "Do you know the way?"

"I do now. I just thought… never mind. First, we must escape the draugr."

A chill swept over me, even though the day was warm. My guide, who seemed so sure, was confused. I could not forget the madness that gnawed at the Berserkers at all times. Ragnar seemed so big and solid, so powerful. *I wanted power too, once. Long ago.* A warrior at the height of his strength. He'd submitted himself to a witch's spell with his pack, and become a Berserker. With his strength came rage. Rage and madness.

As we hurried on, I clutched at a leather strap criss-crossing Ragnar's back. It was slick with sweat but warm and real under my fingers. If the Corpse King was playing tricks, my own mind was suspect. If it was simply the Berserker madness, and Ragnar chose to turn on me, I was lost anyway. Nothing would save me from this Berserker if his grip on reality snapped.

And yet, for some reason, being close to him gave me comfort. My feelings would pass, I was sure, as soon as we were out of danger. Or as soon as Ragnar said something to provoke me.

As soon as my fingers closed on the leather, Ragnar halted. I waited for him to chastise me, but he only reached back and transferred my hand to another strap at his left side, opposite his sword. For a moment, his fingers lingered, closing over mine. He squeezed, once.

Then the moment passed and we moved on, deeper into the dark forest. I stuck close to my captor. My would-be protector. I moved with him, clinging like a shadow to his side. We breathed as one.

How quickly I'd aligned myself to him. It would be enough to marvel at, if I were not so busy trying to stay alive. Stay alive—and then escape.

We passed another thicket, but before we could break free of it to the relatively easy way of the road, Ragnar grabbed my arm. "Get down." We tucked ourselves behind the boulders, listening to the trudging sound of many wooden limbs striking the earth in tandem.

He peered over the boulder. I peeked around mine as well. The sight sent chills to my bones.

The draugr marched forward, lines upon lines filling the

road. Rows and rows of the undead. The scent of clove and grave clothes hung over them all in a seething fog.

"So many. Where do they come from?" My voice shook a little.

"You don't want to know." His head wove back and forth, searching for a good route.

"An army," I whispered. "He's building an army."

"He has been for some time," Ragnar agreed. He squinted at me as if he was wondering how I knew. I hoped he would not ask me. I knew the Corpse King was building an army because I had seen it. The dreams I had were visions he had planted in my mind.

I shuddered, drawing my cloak around me, pressing a hand to the dagger between my breast. "How will we pass them?"

"We cannot. We cannot attract attention. We will go around."

"Ragnar. The farm. The families." I clutched his shoulder. "We must help them."

"No, little runaway. There is no help for them."

I put a hand to my stomach.

He tucked a finger under my chin, raising it until I met his stormy blue eyes. "Courage now. You will need it." He took my hand, threading his huge fingers through mine. "Head down," he ordered. "Run."

I did his bidding, staring at the tips of my boots as we went, letting Ragnar lead the way.

We broke out of the forest and ran alongside another rock wall, then crossed a stream—he scooped me up in his arms to leap over it. I knotted my hands behind his neck and didn't ask to be let down.

"That should help," he muttered to himself. But we followed the stream to another road, and there, trampling the worn grass, were more undead.

"Ragnar," I whispered and pointed up the road. The draugr moved with animated jerks, as if controlled by a distant puppet master. The ones I'd seen in the forest before were skeletal, their skin hanging off their bones. These were fresh. They looked like men with unusually grey skin. They bore shining weapons—swords and shields. And they marched in formation up the road. In lines, like a true army.

Ragnar cursed. "Hang on." And the world blurred.

I dug my fingernails into his neck, ducking my face close to his skin so I could surround myself with his sweaty scent. This was Berserker speed—faster than any man could run. If anyone could free us from the Corpse King's lands, Ragnar could.

But again and again, every route he tried, we were met with more draugr. Marching in rows up the roads. Staggering in unruly lines at the base of a hill. Ranging through the forest, leaving a greasy stench in their wake.

Finally, Ragnar put me down behind a pile of boulders and pulled me to crouch beside him. "We're hemmed in."

Even though he'd run at Berserker speed for hours in the noonday sun, he wasn't even panting hard.

"They are following us. Somehow." His brow furrowed and he swiveled to me. "They must scent you. Or..." He raised his hand and clutched at the front of my gown. I gasped but he tugged out the dagger before I could stop him.

The moonstone did not glow as it sometimes did. As it had last night. It was a mere milky stone, dull in his hand.

"The dagger, it's calling to them," he said suddenly. And before I could stop him, he wrenched it forward, breaking the leather thong around my neck and tossing it, cord and all, into the mud.

"No," I cried, but he was already dragging me along. I couldn't fight. If I tried to tug my hand away, I'd wrench my arm from its socket, and Ragnar would only carry me again.

I kept looking back but the moonstone was gone from view.

"You don't understand," I said in a broken voice. "I needed that."

"Why?"

I shook my head. Whatever spell was upon my lips wouldn't let me speak of my quest. At least, not to Ragnar.

Plant the moonstone in the heart of the Corpse King's power, the crone told me as she handed me the dagger with the moonstone affixed to the pommel. *To do so, you must plunge the dagger into the enemy's heart.*

Now all was lost, and I couldn't even explain. "You made me lose it."

"That weapon drew the cursed ones, the undead. It called to them."

"No matter. I am cursed myself. The witches told me." Apparently, I could speak of this part.

Ragnar stopped so quickly, I bumped into him. "What do you mean?" His blue eyes searched my face.

"I don't…" How could I explain? "I bear a mark upon me." I brushed my forehead where the crone had touched me. "It links me to… him." I lowered my voice. I did not want to invoke the Corpse King's name so close to his army.

Now Ragnar's eyes were flaring bright. "What is the best way to break it?" His voice was rough.

I squeezed his forearm. *Please, don't turn into the beast.* "I don't know." I was suddenly so tired. Fog rose in my mind. My thoughts were sluggish, cobwebbed. My skin turned clammy and peppered with goosebumps, even though I'd been sweating in the humidity before.

…toys with the weather, with life and death of every creature. But by far his favorite target is the mind.

"Something's wrong." My voice was slurred.

"Rosalind?"

"You must leave me. There is no hope for me. I will never be free."

"No," he growled. "I will never leave you." Wind gusted around us, and Ragnar pulled me close. A rough thumb brushed my cheek. His eyes no longer gleamed the bright color of the beast. But they were still brilliant, blue as a summer sky. "The mage is in your mind. Don't let him win."

I gripped Ragnar's arm, fighting the swooning sensation. The firm muscle bunched under my palm was the only thing solid. "How can I stop him?"

"You are strong enough to defeat him." His large hand clamped on my neck, squeezing. He pressed his forehead against mine. "Come back to me, Rosalind."

I opened my mouth, gasping like a fish on a riverbank. The air was too thick to breathe, filled with a scent of grave spices. "He's here. The Corpse King is here."

Ragnar wrenched away. Light flashed on his upraised blades.

"No," I choked out. "You cannot fight him that way."

Beyond Ragnar, a thick mist crept forward. Then a wall of rotting limbs broke from the grey fog. The undead had found us.

The trap had closed. We were going to die.

"I can fight them," Ragnar called over his shoulder, still brandishing his axe and long knife, "but you must stay alive. Promise me you'll fight." He took his eyes from the enemy's front line long enough to bend down and growl in my ear. "Promise."

His voice seemed far away. I raised my arms as if I could swim back to him. "I promise."

"Good." His beard scratched my cheek.

More wind blew up, cutting through the thick fog. Suddenly, I could breathe again.

"Storm coming." I pointed to the dark clouds boiling

overhead. The wind picked up, tearing at my gown. I clutched at the dagger around my neck, only to remember it was gone.

"The mage likes his tricks." Ragnar maneuvered me backwards until we were both crouched behind a tree. "Hide here," he said. "Wait for me. But when you see a way through, run. I will clear a path for you."

"But…" I tugged on the straps crisscrossing his back, pulling him back.

"Yes?"

I licked my lips, staring into his fierce eyes.

One Berserker can best a few corpses. But an army of them? Eventually, they would cut him down. I had a few bespelled weapons in my pouch, but too few to do any good. Not enough to destroy even a third of this force.

Behind Ragnar, the mist and forces advanced. "They're coming."

"Rosalind," Ragnar said softly, as if we were alone. "Do you fear for me?"

I bit my lip and ducked my head, but he caught my chin.

"Rosalind," he purred. "Do you care for me?" His sapphire eyes flashed.

"I care that you return safely." I pushed him away. "I don't want to die."

"If we are separated, you needn't fear. I will come for you. I will find you." He bowed his head over me and kissed my forehead.

Then he rose up with a roar.

"You think you can best me? Come, take me." Lightning flashed as he raced towards the enemy.

I fell back behind the tree, touching my forehead where he had kissed me. His lips had covered the mark where the witch had touched my forehead. And then I remembered what else she'd said.

We will send help, the crone told me. *Do not allow yourself to be separated.*

"Wait—" I whispered. The mark of Ragnar's kiss burned on my skin as if it was a tangible thing. But Ragnar was gone. I could not be separated from him. Even if I wasn't sure whether the witches had sent him to help, I could not fail again.

And if we fell, we'd fall together.

Out in the glade, there was a roar, and the clanging of axe against blade. I cringed then stopped. If this was to be my end, I would not grovel in the dirt. I would face it on two feet.

Ragnar was a blur of motion. He'd charged forward until the mist reached to his knees, and used his axe and knife to cut through the draugr. The bodies fell like scarecrows before a scythe.

But there were too many, and as he rushed forward, the lurching corpses filled in the gap behind him.

"Ragnar!" I screamed, and he whirled, slicing through more bodies. The beast had taken over now, turning his fingers to claws. His weapons spun, ripping through corpse after corpse. He tossed his axe, and it tore through several foes. They fell into the mist, and he grabbed a few more bodies and tossed them on the pile.

But more draugr rushed in to replace the fallen.

I clenched my fists, waiting for my chance to run. I'd make Ragnar escape with me. The wind picked up, stirring the mist, pushing it away.

And then I saw it clearly—behind me, emerging from the forest. More draugr. I pushed away from the tree I'd been hiding behind and raced to another, stumbling over the broken corpses Ragnar had left in his wake.

I reached a second tree right as lightning struck, flooding the glade with light.

"Rosalind," Ragnar bellowed. Smoke billowed from the ground as if the very earth were on fire. He leapt across the pile of corpses to my side. I pressed my face to his chest and gasped for air.

"What is happening?" I was coughing on the scent of magic in one moment, and finding relief in the next, as the wind blew fresh on my face.

"Come on." Ragnar helped me stagger forward. We had to leave the glade. But the flames were licking along our path— draugr bursting into flame.

"Look out!" I shrieked. Overhead was a roaring darkness, a swirling, black tunnel of wind-whipped clouds. "What is that thing?"

"I've seen such things upon the water," Ragnar muttered. "A spout of water connecting the sea and sky. But never on land. It is the Corpse King's doing."

"What do we do?" The darkness was almost upon us. The black clouds blotted out the sun.

"Hang onto me." His voice was muffled by my hair. His broad arms secured me against him.

The roaring sound was almost upon us. But the closer it got, the more it sounded like a man's shout.

I stretched to my tiptoes. Over Ragnar's shoulder, lightning struck the ground again and again. The flashes cleared from my eyes and left a shadowy shape. I blinked, and realized the shape was a dark-cloaked man with his hands outstretched as if he could float on the wind. His long fingers caressed the mist, and it billowed away. His dark hair floated around his clean-shaven face.

Above our heads, the black tunnel of roaring sound was gone. The air crackled with energy. Like the lightning was living and breathing among us, licking along my skin.

The man looked over… and winked at me.

Behind him, a line of draugr appeared, creeping forward as one, with swords outstretched.

"Look out," I screamed to the newcomer. He turned slowly towards the enemy, his cloak rippling in the wind.

Lightning shot from the sky, hitting one of the corpses and setting it afire. The fire spread along the front line of the draugrs' ranks.

"Thank you, brother!" the newcomer called. He took a step forward, and lightning struck the ground before him. "Thor's balls," he swore. He held his cloak closed with one hand as he shook his opposite fist at the sky. "Are very tiny," he muttered under his breath. Then his head snapped up and he looked at me. "Behind you!"

Ragnar thrust me aside. While we'd waited, draugr had advanced on all sides. Ragnar whirled, grabbed up his long knife and dipped, cutting the corpses' legs from under them.

A blazing limb came flying through the air. Ragnar barely dodged it. "You fool," he shouted to the warrior who'd thrown it. But the makeshift torch landed on the fallen draugr and flared up into a shining wall of fire.

I covered my mouth against the stench, but the new warrior was grinning. "What fun," he cackled. "Come, let us make a pyre!"

Ragnar ran his hand down his beard. I stepped closer to him.

"Is he a Berserker?" I asked in a low voice. We both watched the newcomer dance from corpse to corpse, tossing them into a giant pile.

"I think so." Ragnar's forehead creased. "I think I recognize him."

Flames shot up from the growing bonfire. The dark-cloaked warrior was frowning at the ground. He skipped sideways and thrust his hand between two fallen corpses, then held up Ragnar's axe. "Did you lose this?"

Ragnar held out his hand. The newcomer grinned—and threw the axe. The weapon spun slowly, end over end, the broad head flashing as it cut through the air. Straight towards Ragnar's chest.

At the last second, Ragnar jerked aside, half staggering, half falling backwards. The axe whistled past him and hit one of the undead who'd snuck up behind us. The blade cracked the creature's chest. A vile smell burst out of the putrid flesh, and the body fell in a clanking pile of bones, the dry, rotted corpse animated no more.

Ragnar caught his balance and touched his hair. One of his braids fell into the dirt. "Well thrown," he grunted, reaching down to retrieve his axe.

"You're welcome, brother." The second warrior grinned.

"What's your name?" Ragnar called.

"Loki," the man called back. "And you are Ragnar. I'm here to help."

Movement in the trees caught my eye. "Ragnar, there are more of them." I picked up my skirts, scuttling to the side of the glade where I might be out of the way of the fight. Behind me, the pyre of corpses burned.

Ragnar gestured with his axe towards the advancing corpses. "Shall we fight?"

"Oh yes." Loki shrugged off his cloak, letting the dark shape flutter to the ground. Without it, the warrior was totally naked. Dark markings swirled over his broad chest—tattoos, and bits of mud. He tilted his head back and sniffed the burning air. "It's a good day for a fight!"

Shaking his head, Ragnar tossed his long knife to Loki. The weapon spun end over end but somehow the Berserker snatched it out of the air. "Let us harvest this crop of bones."

The two warriors stood back to back. Loki was almost as tall as Ragnar, but leaner. His powerful body was lithe and tanned, and while Ragnar bore the weals and marks of many scars, Loki's skin was smooth.

I gripped my skirts and prayed to no one. *Please, please, let them make it out.* If they fell, I would be captured. I would not be able to escape without them.

The Corpse King's forces advanced with jerky movements, closing in from all sides. The mist was rising again, blending with the stinking smoke from the burning fallen. I clapped a hand to my face, swaying on my feet.

The line of animated corpses rippled like the body of a snake. The draugr at the head lunged—and Ragnar cut it down. Metal flashed in the fog, their weapons rising and falling in rhythm. The warriors' movements became a blur.

They fought like a whirlwind. The bodies of the enemy fell aside, writhing.

One severed limb fell near me, still moving. I kicked it into the fire, and dragged my cloak over the lower half of my face to repel the stench. I'd lost sight of the warriors, but Ragnar's roars and Loki's singsong laugh told me where they were.

The air all around was grey, like the day had dropped a cloak over this glade. Smoke and mist melded into an opaque wall. The sounds grew distant. I staggered, my eyes stinging.

A firm hand caught my arm. "Rosalind." Ragnar drew me close. "Are you all right?"

"Still standing," I choked out. "Is it over?"

"Almost." The sounds of the battle had quieted. The Berserker guided me to the forest edge and handed me the waterskin. I drank some, and splashed a bit on my face to clear my eyes.

"We survived," Ragnar murmured. His big body blocked me from the battle site.

"I see that." Ignoring my slowing heartbeat and the heat

rising between us, I pushed at him so I could see what had become of the enemy.

The mist had blown away, and the fire died to bitter ash.

There were barely any more draugr left standing. A few twitched on the ground, still animated and trying to rise. The naked warrior Loki skipped over to them and cut them down.

The wind picked up and I drew my cloak around me. I had been so worried about Ragnar and the outcome of the battle, then relieved by Loki's arrival. But now, there were two warriors I had to escape from.

Ragnar's shadow fell over me. Now that we were safe, he would not leave my side.

Ah well. A small part of me wanted to give up, curl into the giant warrior, and let him carry me away.

Ragnar was smiling, as if he could sense my weakness.

"Fortunate that Loki was here to help you," I said tartly. Even if some part of me wanted Ragnar, he'd not find me easy prey.

But Ragnar only shook his head, grinning as if nothing I said could prick him. "It was a fine fight."

"Aye," Loki agreed. He bore a lazy half smile, his eyes heavy-lidded, as if he'd been dreaming. "A fine fight," he repeated drunkenly.

"Well done, brother," Ragnar called. "Did the Alphas send you?"

"Not them," Loki murmured. He found his cloak and used it to clean his blade. In the fight, he'd somehow ended up with Ragnar's axe.

"No?" Ragnar frowned.

"But I do have a message for Rosalind." Loki swiveled his head to me. *Run,* he mouthed clearly, and jerked his chin towards the forest—the opposite direction to the way Ragnar was taking me.

I gaped at Loki, and he winked at me. Then he swiveled, snapped his arm back, and threw the axe straight at Ragnar.

This time, the weapon spun end over end, and Ragnar twisted out of the way too late.

The axe struck him full in the chest. Blood spurted and I screamed. Ragnar staggered back.

Before I could rush to Ragnar's side, Loki grabbed my arm, his long, pale fingers like a vise.

I yelped, and swatted at him.

"Be still." He shook me, his face grim. One eye was brown, so dark it was almost black like a raven's, and the other was green as a laurel leaf. His head dipped so his lips touched my ear. A wintergreen scent washed over me, so strong, it was like a cool breath on my cheek. I tasted magic. Strong magic. "The witches sent me."

The ground shifted under my feet. I stumbled. "What?"

But Loki had turned back to Ragnar.

"Traitor," Ragnar snarled. He lay on the ground, blood flowing from his chest. With a grunt, he grabbed the axe head and yanked it out. Fresh blood poured from the gash, soaking the ground until he lay in a pool of red.

But he was a Berserker. Soon, the wound would heal.

Loki released me and approached Ragnar with his hands outstretched. "Come now, brother."

Ragnar's eyes flashed gold. His shoulders were changing, bulking up, sprouting black fur. "You are no brother."

Loki shrugged. His head swung back to me, his smile dropping away. "What are you waiting for? Run!" He shooed me with a long hand. "I'll keep him from following."

Mouth hanging open, I picked up my skirts, and took a few steps towards the forest.

"Rosalind," Ragnar bellowed. Blood flowed between his fingers, but he seemed not to care.

Loki stepped between me and the warrior on the ground. "It will be all right."

He reached down, stole Ragnar's long knife out of his leg sheath, and started tossing it up and down.

"Let's play a new game," Loki said. "You with your axe, me with your knife."

"I'll kill you." Ragnar sat up. The gash on his chest was smaller, his flesh knitting together before our very eyes.

"Sounds fun," Loki said to Ragnar. He turned and shooed me again. *Go on*, he mouthed. I took a few more steps, but stopped between two birch trees.

"Don't hurt him," I whispered.

"I won't," Loki said, and turned away, shaking his head, still wearing a wild grin.

I fled into the forest, Ragnar's roars chasing me through the trees.

 osalind

THE FOREST WELCOMED me on my newfound quest. I had no dagger to guide me, but my steps were certain. I knew I was headed towards the Corpse King. The growing sense of dread in my breast was a sure sign.

At least there were no draugr in my way anymore. There would be more ahead, but I could not think about that. I could only take one step at a time.

I shook my head as I reviewed the past day and night's events.

We will send help, the witches had told me. They'd sent Loki. The Alphas sent Ragnar. And I was caught in the middle.

I was still on the quest, but I had no dagger and no moonstone.

The moonstone is the weapon. It is the source of power and can be used to bind him.

And Ragnar had thrown it away. I needed it back, but what hope did I have of finding it?

"The witches said they'd send help," I grumbled to the oak trees. "They also told me once I found it, I should not allow myself to be separated from it."

I halted in my steps, tearing at my hair. My braid had long ago come undone. I was hungry, dirty, and tired. Not to mention, I smelled like draugr.

I had no moonstone, no help, and no hope.

Why should I even go on?

"I give up," I announced to the sky peeping through the leafy canopy. I should return to Ragnar and let him take me to Berserker mountain. Cower there with the rest of the spaewives until the Corpse King came to destroy us all.

"But where's the fun in that?" someone drawled behind me. I yelped and whirled around.

Loki stood in the shadow of a great oak, grinning at me. He was dressed in black, from the top of his dark head to the tips of his boots. No cloak this time. I did not ask where he got his clothes from.

He spread his hands in greeting. "Happy to see me?"

I shook my head and turned my back on him to hide the part of me that was a little relieved.

He fell into step beside me, matching his long stride to mine.

"Where are we going?" he asked after a few minutes.

I said nothing and kept walking back the way I'd come: the opposite direction of the Corpse King's lair. Each step lifted a little of the dread.

"So silent? Ragnar said you would not stop talking."

Ragnar. I stopped short. "Where is Ragnar?"

"Back there." The warrior waved a careless hand.

"You left him?"

"Of course," he said. "I was rescuing you."

I swallowed the image of Ragnar on the ground in a blossoming pool of his own blood. "Is he… Did it…"

Loki waited patiently for me to form my question. His eyes really were two different colors, though the brown one looked more normal, no longer an eerie black.

"Did you kill him?" I finally asked.

"Did you care for him? I was under the impression he had taken you against your will."

I blushed. "He did," I said slowly.

Loki cocked his head, squinting at me—not passing judgment, but as if he could see what I was thinking. "He'll be all right," he said finally. "You don't need to worry about him."

"I wasn't worried," I snapped before I could stop the lie.

"Whatever you say, my lady. But now it seems I must kidnap you, for you are going the wrong way." He pointed east. "That is the way your quest lies."

"I cannot continue," I said. "There's nothing more for me to do." I would not return to Ragnar or Berserker Mountain. I would go far away, where neither Berserkers nor witches could find me. I would find my own way. If I traveled long enough, far enough, fast enough, perhaps I could find a land where the Corpse King did not exist.

But I would never escape the guilt.

You have a choice, the witches had told me, but I didn't really. Even though I hated the world and everyone in it, how could I let it burn?

"Did you lose your way?" Loki asked.

I rubbed my forehead. "It's no matter. I lost the moonstone and the dagger. My quest is for naught."

"Ah, then you might be interested in what I discovered lying in the mud."

He pulled out the dagger with its thin blade. The moonstone glittered in the hilt.

Just like that, what I needed was there in his hand.

I reached for it and he pulled it away. From his weapon belt, he tugged out two more daggers—small and silver like the moonstone one— from their sheaths, and started to juggle them.

I watched with my hands fisted at my sides. He was too tall, his reach too long, for me to grab the moonstone dagger.

"I found what you need. What will you give me for it?"

I crossed my arms over my chest. "My undying gratitude."

Loki plucked each dagger from the air, one by one, and sheathed them again. The one with the moonstone was the last. He dangled it high above my head. "How about a kiss?"

I pressed my lips together.

His grin turned sly. "Have you ever enjoyed a kiss?"

I looked away, remembering Ragnar's body pressing me into the leaves, the heat and weight of him as the beast.

"A shame that you had no enjoyment of this life before you take leave of it," Loki murmured.

I stiffened. "So I'm going to die?"

"You act like you are." He threw himself down on the thick carpet of leaves, leaning against a moss-covered log. "I will give you the dagger, but I wish a boon."

"What is it you wish?"

"I wish to kiss you. Whenever I want, as many times as I want." There was a twinkle in his right eye—the green one. The dark one opposite merely unsettled me.

Still, he was handsome as a fallen angel. He sprawled on the forest floor, looking as regal as a prince reclining on furs. Even after the dusty battle, his clothes were pristine.

Something in me ached to go to him. I pushed the feeling away. "No."

He tossed the dagger in the air. It turned end over end. He plucked it out of the air, pulled it close to kiss the pommel stone, and tossed it up again.

My toe twitched in my boot. A few steps and I could plant

my foot in his gut, but then what? I needed to get that dagger back. "I will kiss you. Once."

Loki caught the dagger, closing his palm around the blade. I winced on his behalf, but when he opened his hand, his palm was unscathed.

"You will kiss me? Willingly?" His odd eyes glittered.

"Yes." I crossed my arms over my bodice. "I've never kissed a man willingly. You will be the first."

"I'm flattered. Are you sure you're willing?"

"Yes."

"All right then." He rolled to his feet in one smooth movement, and continued stretching up while his hands drew up his jerkin. He tossed it away, giving me a close view of his perfect chest. The last time I saw him, he was naked and smeared with mud. Now his skin was clean and free of any tattoos.

Perhaps I had imagined them.

"Like what you see?" Loki winked at me. His hands were busy undoing his belt, the one that held his sheathed weapons.

I held up a hand to stop him. "What are you doing?"

"Removing my clothes." He slid the belt off and tossed it and his weapons onto the fallen jerkin. "You said you would kiss me; you didn't say where."

To forestall any more conversation, I leaned in, planted a hand on his chest and, trying to ignore the firm and smooth muscles under my palm and his wintergreen scent, popped up to my tiptoes and pecked Loki's cheek.

I backed away to face his baleful expression.

"Ah, a sisterly kiss," he said flatly. "Well done. I've kissed my enemies with more enthusiasm."

I rolled my eyes. "You did not specify enthusiasm. Only that I'd kiss you willingly."

"Yes, I suppose you did it willingly. Here then, a deal's a

deal." He flicked his wrist and tossed the dagger to the ground at my feet. I kept my eyes on him as I picked it up, expecting a trick. Loki swiped his jerkin and belt off the ground and redressed himself.

I sat down on the log, turning the dagger over in my lap. There was no flash of blue light. The dagger looked ordinary without the precious stone.

Loki had tricked me. He'd given me the dagger but not the moonstone.

"What have you done?"

His cheeks curved slowly. He showed me his empty hand, then turned it over and the stone appeared briefly between each finger before he flicked it into the air.

"I need that." I clenched my jaw before I begged for it.

"New bargain." Loki kept tossing the stone. "This time, I kiss you."

Would this never end? I held up a finger. "You may give me a kiss in exchange for it. Once."

"Very well." He seated himself smoothly on the log beside me.

I offered him my cheek. He leaned in, and pretended to overbalance and fall in my lap.

"No." I pushed him, but he pulled me off the log and onto my back, where he pinned me and started drawing up my skirts.

"What are you doing?"

"We bargained for a kiss. I forgot to specify where you could kiss me," he paused, "but so did you. So I may kiss you where I please."

He inched up my skirt. My breath caught. My heartbeat ricocheted in my chest.

My fists gripped the folds of my skirt, whether to pull it up or push it down, I did not know.

Loki slid my skirts up higher, all laughing looks gone

now. His face was somber as a priest in church as he exposed my legs. Underneath my heavier dress, I was clad only in a light shift. He slipped his hand under this, too, clasping my bare leg. His cool, wintergreen scent blew over me.

"Beautiful," he murmured. His touch was light as the brush of a butterfly's wing. My bodice became too tight for my breath.

He took an ankle and stroked it, studying the binding Ragnar had given me. "He cared for you then?"

"He did."

Light fingers traced up my legs, tickling the soft golden down lining my calves. Loki's hand ventured higher to cup my knee. The joint was strangely ticklish. I wriggled, and Loki smiled. "I would kiss here. But there is a more sacred place."

"Where?" I asked, because I could not take my eyes from his.

"Here." He cupped between my legs. My cunny pulsed against his palm, throbbing like a second heartbeat. "May I kiss you here, Rosalind?"

I wanted nothing more than for him to kiss me. "A deal's a deal," I whispered back.

"One kiss? Will it be enough?"

I swallowed. Sweat sheened my skin, all over.

He chuckled. "Not yet. Another time." He flipped down the hem of my gown, covering my body, leaving my cunny bereft.

He planted a hand by my hip and leaned in to kiss my mouth. His wintergreen scent washed over me—his magic as pungent as mint, and as intoxicating as mead.

Before our lips touched, I struck his shoulder. He was bigger, stronger, but I caught him off guard and he tipped back enough for me to scramble to my feet.

My chest heaved, rage and arousal surging, washing back

into each other until I would burst with emotion. My cheeks burned.

Loki came to his feet, laughing, and I struck him again. "Curse you," I gritted out. "Leave me alone."

I spun around and strode from him, tears blurring my way. My cunny throbbed. Damn my body for betraying me.

Damn him. Damn the moonstone and the dagger.

I wanted him to touch me. I was bare and open to him, and he rejected me?

If I could kill him, I would.

"Rosalind." He caught up with me, but his speech still lilted with laughter. "Odin's beard, slow down."

"No." I changed directions, blundering into a briar bush in my haste to get away. Thorns tore at my skirts and I ripped at them, thrashing as the briars caught my arms and hair.

"Stop," Loki ordered. "You'll hurt yourself." He stepped in and freed me, his long fingers picking away the thorns and smoothing the skin, checking for blood.

"Get away from me." I ducked away. How was I going to escape him?

I didn't need to worry. A loud battle cry rang through the woods.

Loki half turned. A giant shape blurred out of the forest, hit Loki with full force, and bore him to the ground. The ground shook from the impact, and a boulder flew out of the way.

I backed deeper into the thicket. When it came to two Berserkers fighting, it was wise to cower well out of the way.

Somehow, Loki wrestled himself free. Ragnar bellowed as his opponent escaped.

"Loki! Come back here and fight."

"Again?" Loki danced backwards, pulling leaves from his hair. "Don't you tire of me beating you?"

"You cheated," Ragnar snarled.

Loki held out his arms. His brown eye was raven black again. "I am a trickster."

Ragnar held out a cautioning hand in my direction. "Rosalind, step away. He is mad. He thinks he is a god." Ragnar planted himself between me and the dark-haired warrior, and gripped his axe. "But he bleeds like a man."

"Like a Berserker." Loki buffed his fingernails against his fine jerkin, looking bored. "You're upsetting our runaway. Let's put down our weapons and settle this fairly."

"You do not fight fairly."

"Fine. You keep your weapon. But I shall set aside mine." He dropped his belt, the one that sheathed his many-sized daggers. Almost as an afterthought, he tossed the moonstone to me. I caught it, grasping it tight though it buzzed against my palm. The blue light glowed between my fingers.

I ducked behind a tree to check if I really held the stone in my palm. The buzzing was real. The light was real. Loki had actually helped me.

This time.

"Leave us, Berserker," Loki was commanding Ragnar. "This doesn't concern you."

"I will kill you and leave your body to feed the ravens," Ragnar growled. "Rosalind is mine."

"If you won't listen, I'll pound it into your thick skull."

I slipped the stone and the dagger into my pouch.

Enough. I had the moonstone, I had the dagger. Loki would keep Ragnar from following me. With any luck, Ragnar would keep Loki from me too.

A roar signaled that Ragnar had lost his patience with Loki's baiting and attacked again. A boom and a great oak tree rocked from the impact. Leaves rained down.

I peeked around a laurel bush. Loki and Ragnar were

locked in a struggle, both standing, their boots digging furrows into the leafy ground as they gripped each other in an almost brotherly embrace. Ragnar's face was red with exertion. Loki looked bored, but his boots were slowly slipping backwards.

This was my chance. I gripped my cloak tight to keep it from snagging on more briars, and edged further away from the warriors.

"Rosalind!" Ragnar's call made me pause. But I could not stay for him. There was no logical reason why I'd even want to.

"A kiss!" Loki cried with manic cheer. He stopped pushing, letting Ragnar fall forward into him. Loki hauled the blond Berserker up and gripped both sides of his face.

"What?" Ragnar grunted in horror, his blue eyes widening as Loki's lips descended on his.

I didn't wait to see how passionately Loki kissed another. Clapping my hand over my mouth to stifle a laugh, I ducked behind the laurels again. Another roar shook the woods behind me as I ran away.

* * *

Ragnar

"You fool," I shouted at Loki for the fiftieth time. I would deny he was a Berserker if I didn't remember him from the pack. My memory wasn't what it once was but I seemed to remember a warrior with one eye brown and one eye green. He may have been strange, but he'd never committed treason like this. When I reported him to the Alphas, they'd tear him apart.

But I planned to cut him to pieces first.

I scrubbed at my lips to destroy the feeling of Loki's touch. "Why would you kiss me?"

"Don't say you didn't enjoy it." Loki pursed his lips.

The world turned red. I attacked, and he threw himself out of the way, diving into a somersault and rolling to bounce to his feet.

"I will kill you," I vowed.

"Not unless I kill you first," he pointed out. "Come and get me," he singsonged, dancing around me.

I raised my axe above my head. A showy move. I attacked straight on, but at the last, I feinted, dropping my axe to cut across his middle.

Loki jerked back and my axe missed his midriff by a hair's breadth.

"Stand still, you fool," I bellowed.

"Like you did when I kissed you?" Loki winked.

I lunged and he danced backwards. "Shut up and fight!"

"And let you kill me?"

"At least you'd die like a man."

"I can't die. Not yet," he said. "The gods haven't willed it. I must fulfill my quest." He put a hand over his heart and bowed. In the middle of a battle, he bowed.

"I will send you back to your makers. You will fail your quest."

"I must not fail," he said sadly. "If I die this time, it will be the final time. I must atone for my sins." He bowed again. "But first, we must find our quarry. Do you know where our little runaway is?"

I stopped stalking him and straightened. "Rosalind?"

The glade was empty, but when I raised my head there was a hint of her scent on the breeze.

I cursed. "Thor's balls."

"Are not as big as you would think," Loki quipped.

"Will you shut up?" I growled, and marched off in the

direction where Rosalind had gone. I must find her, and I would. There was no one else to keep her safe in these woods. None other than Loki, and I didn't trust him. "Quit talking like you're a god."

"But I'm not a god," Loki said. "Not anymore."

I tugged my beard and rubbed my brow. Loki mimicked my movements, tugging on his chin because he had no beard. What sort of Berserker shaves his beard?

My head hurt. Was Loki the Berserker I remembered, always this crazy?

"You're addled in the head," I grumbled.

"Better than being addled in the bed," Loki singsonged again.

"Shut up, and run."

I dodged around trees, trying to out-distance him. But no matter how fast I ran, Loki was at my elbow, his long dark hair flying in the wind as he cackled like a man gone mad.

* * *

ROSALIND

THE SUN WAS SETTING when I realized I was walking in circles. I'd passed the same crop of boulders and birch grove twice.

I held the moonstone in my outstretched palm. In the past, it had lit the way, but now its surface remained dull. Was I closer to the Corpse King's land or farther away?

Since I'd met with Ragnar, nothing had gone right. When I'd been with him, it seemed like the army of undead was herding us back towards the Corpse King. I could feel his presence growing closer in my head, but no clear guidance to help me go forward. Only a reluctance to move at all. The very ground seemed to suck at my boots.

I clutched at the dagger I'd rehung around my throat, and slumped against a tree. Why should I continue this quest? Loki had given back the moonstone and dagger, but what use was a dagger against a powerful mage?

The witches had said they would send me help, but so far, I'd been beset by two warriors: one mad, one determined to thwart my quest.

I picked a direction at random and started walking, only to halt when a shadow fell across my path.

Ragnar stepped from behind a tree. I hadn't heard him approach. "Rosalind."

I squawked and dashed away, but Loki was there to catch me.

"Once again, you're going the wrong way," he murmured in my ear, and pushed me back into Ragnar's arms.

"Got you," the blue-eyed warrior said.

"Let me go!" I pushed at Ragnar and he clamped his arms around me. I let my weight sag, then tried to kick between his legs.

"She's fighting you," Loki observed.

"Shut up and help," Ragnar grunted. I couldn't angle myself enough to kick between his legs, so I stomped on his feet until he lifted me clear off the ground.

"I prefer to watch." Loki had seated himself against a log, lounging back with his fingers laced behind his head. "You can tire each other out, then I can grab her and be on my way."

"You can try." Ragnar wrestled me, holding my wrists lightly as I tried to gouge his eyes out.

"We cannot keep fighting over her," Loki commented. "It makes no sense."

"It is good that you see the truth of it," Ragnar said. "So let me have her, and I will take her to the Alphas. Keep my way clear."

"No, no," Loki said. "The witches have a different plan. Rosalind is the key to defeating the Corpse King."

Ragnar's grip slackened and I got loose, dashing a few steps—only for Loki to catch me again.

"Be still, little runaway." Loki held me fast with little effort.

Ragnar's brow was creased. "She cannot defeat the Corpse King," he spoke over my head to Loki. "The Corpse King is a mage of great power. What chance does a young woman stand against his evil?"

"Nevertheless, the witches have spoken." Loki locked me against him, my back to his front, and nuzzled my cheek. I growled and tried to elbow him in the gut.

"The witches are as crazy as you are," Ragnar said, his eyes flashing yellow. "I will rescue Rosalind, and I will not be denied."

"I will go with neither of you," I bellowed, and wrenched free. I backed away, looking wildly about for a way to escape. Both Berserkers stalked me, moving slowly, as if they had all the time in the world to catch me.

"We need to find a way to come to peaceful terms," Loki said to Ragnar, keeping his eyes on me. "What do you say to a game of stones?"

"This is foolishness," I muttered, and dived for the forest. Two hands grasped each of my arms and pulled me back. I cried out.

"We will wrench her apart at this rate," Loki reasoned. "Let us tie her up and then we'll decide what to do."

That is how I found myself tied to a tree, bound upright, with ropes crossing over my chest. I leaned back against the bark, my hair in my face and my feet throbbing. I was so tired.

"Poor sweet thing," Loki said, leaning on the tree trunk beside me, his face close to mine. "Let me help." He stroked my blonde tangles back, combing out the leaves, rubbing his fingers over my scalp.

"Will you not untie me?" I asked tiredly. My head throbbed but Loki's touch and his cool magic scent seemed to chase the tightness in my temples away.

"Not until we decide what to do with you," Ragnar called from where he was building a fire.

"I promise not to run."

"You made that promise before." Ragnar stood, dusting off his hands. He leaned against the tree trunk on my opposite side. Two Berserkers, one dark, one fair, both at odds and united in purpose against me.

I sighed and let my head fall back. No use fighting.

Loki cocked his head to the side. "What if we untie her—but first make sure she's too tired to run?"

Ragnar stroked his beard. "It might be possible."

"There are many ways to wear her out," Loki said. The two Berserkers turned their gaze on me, triggering a rush of heat between my legs.

I squeezed my thighs together, but it was no use. Hot liquid leaked down my legs. I blinked as the heavy pall of the Corpse King's magic lifted, the fog lifting, dissipating, curling away like burning leaves. My headache was gone, replaced by the throbbing hunger in my lower belly.

Loki snapped his fingers. "That's it. That is our contest." He waggled his brows at Ragnar. "Whoever makes her climax first, wins."

"Done," Ragnar said, rising and heading towards me, an intent look on his face.

"Wait," Loki and I called at the same time.

Ragnar halted at my side, looming over me. The heat and

scent of him enveloped me. Pinned by the blue fire in his eyes, I quivered in my bonds.

"What?" Ragnar snapped at Loki, without looking away from me.

"You must make her climax but you cannot touch her," Loki said.

"What?"

"You must make her climax but you cannot touch her flesh," Loki repeated, coming to my side. "Your flesh must not touch hers. That is the challenge. Do you agree?"

Ragnar glowered at Loki as if he would attack any moment. The tension between the men on either side of me was too thick to breathe. "Yes," Ragnar said finally.

"Truly?" I gasped. They would make me climax but they would not touch me? How would that be?

Then the men both looked me up and down, undressing me with their eyes. Their gaze left my legs weak. Had I not been bound, I would have fallen.

"Cut her free," Loki said. "Leave her body unbound but tie her arms above her head." Both warriors moved swiftly to make this happen.

They tied me up closer to the campfire, stringing me up with my arms stretched above my head. My wrists were bound and I was trussed from a long rope tied high to the branch. The rest of me was free to twist in the breeze. There was just enough rope to allow my weight to rest on my two feet.

"Comfortable?" Loki asked as he tested the rope above my head.

"Not really," I grumbled, shifting from foot to foot.

"Soon, lovely," he said, cuddling me against him for a moment and stroking my hair back. "Soon."

"No touching," Ragnar growled. He hovered at my opposite side, the heat of him like a furnace baking that side of my body. The searing spice of his anger clashed with Loki's fresh, wintergreen scent.

"Right." Loki stepped back. He braided his own hair back and dusted off his hands. "The contest begins now," he announced.

"I'll go first," Ragnar said. "Since you decided the nature of the challenge."

"Of course." Loki waved his hand and retreated to the campfire, where he crossed his arms and settled in to watch. I glared at him to show my displeasure, but he showed no contrition. Instead, he winked at me.

Ragnar bent closer to me, his expression determined. He circled me slowly. I fought the urge to twist around to keep him in my sights. My spine crawled as if my very flesh knew I was being hunted. He paced back in front of me and stood a few inches away. I felt his gaze on my face.

"You are beautiful," he said.

"I know," I whispered.

Ragnar ducked his head to mine. He was close—so close, his breath fanned my cheek. I closed my eyes. He inhaled deeply. A slight movement, and his stubble would brush my skin.

"No touching," Loki called.

Ragnar's answering growl rumbled deep in his chest, but he didn't turn. He knelt before me and tipped his head close to my skirts, at the apex of my legs. He tilted his head and inhaled again. Scenting me. My cheeks grew warm.

Locking his blue eyes on mine, Ragnar grasped the edge of my gown and drew it upward. My pussy clenched as air hit my lower legs.

"No touching," Loki insisted.

"You said we might not touch her flesh. You did not say we could not touch her clothes."

"True." Loki cocked his head as if considering this. "You

follow the letter of the law, but not the spirit." He broke into a grin. "Well done."

Ragnar rolled his eyes. We shared a private smile before the kneeling warrior got back to tormenting me. Slowly, so slowly, he peeled up my skirts to reveal my white shift. The thin fabric was the only barrier between my flesh and his hot breath.

I shifted from leg to leg.

"Do you want me to hold her?" Loki's voice came from behind. I don't know when he'd moved from the fire, but he had.

"No," Ragnar growled. "Do not touch her."

"It would be over her clothes," Loki said mildly, but he did not move closer, which was wise. At any minute, Ragnar might lose his grip on the beast, and attack.

"Don't worry," Loki said to me, as if he could read my thoughts. "You would survive."

"You're so sure?" I retorted, to hide my unease. This Loki was not what he seemed. "You might worry about your own hide."

"You have concern for my hide?" Loki placed a hand on his heart in mock regard. "I'm touched."

"Shut up," Ragnar muttered, still kneeling before me, his head bowed close to my sex. "You are interrupting my turn."

"So I am," Loki said, but he didn't move away.

"Ignore him," Ragnar ordered me. Still kneeling before me, he turned his head this way and that, and his head was so close to my cunny, his rough beard caught the fabric of my shift and lifted it away. "Spread your legs."

My lips parted but I didn't argue. For some reason, I obeyed. My cunny throbbed in rhythm with my heartbeat. Nectar dripped from my sex, trickling down my inner thighs.

When Ragnar raised his head to me, his eyes were bright gold.

"So lovely," he choked out. "So beautiful." He drew up my shift and bared my sex. My thatch of blonde fur dripped with dew.

"Now that's a sight." Loki stalked back a little ways to admire it. Ragnar seemed transfixed before me. His fingers fumbled with the cloth in his hand. He held up my skirts with one hand as his opposite freed another leather strap, and he bound my dress high around my waist. With both hands free, he planted them on the ground and leaned in, scenting me once again. His beard almost brushed my leg…

"Ragnar," I called. "Ragnar."

He blinked up at me.

"If you touch my flesh, you lose," I told him. At that moment, I did not want him to lose.

He gave a sharp nod. "No touching," he agreed. "No touching." His broad shoulders heaved as he sighed. A gust of his breath hit my sex, and my toes curled in my boots.

He scooted closer on his knees.

"Loki," I called. "May I touch him?"

An evil grin slid across Loki's face. "Hmmm, that is a question." He pretended to ponder, tapping his chin. "No."

"Not even by accident?" I persisted.

At my feet, Ragnar shuddered.

"Do you want him to lose this?" Loki huffed. "Very well, I'll grant you one accident. Just one."

Ragnar did not seem to hear. He leaned in, angling his head so his stubbled chin scraped the blonde tuft between my legs. My heartbeat boomed in my ears.

"Is he touching?" Loki asked me, and Ragnar answered.

"Just my beard. Not my flesh."

"So close to cheating, but not quite." Loki shook his head, but he was grinning. "Very well, I'll allow it."

Ragnar bobbed his head, fully wetting his beard. "Close?" he asked me.

I shuddered, gripping the bonds above my head. My body felt like a fish on a line, captured but not fully taken.

"Close," Ragnar muttered to himself, answering his own question. "But not close enough." He leaned back and slid a long knife from its sheath.

"Ragnar?" My voice trembled as he held the blade close to my cunny.

"Careful," Loki warned.

And Ragnar was careful. He held the knife this way and that, shaving my sex clean of blonde hair. When he was done, goosebumps peppered my newly shorn skin. My cunny felt clean and nude, bared to the air.

This time, when he rubbed his slick beard against my sensitive flesh, sensation burst in my belly, I cried out, gripping the rope above my head to steady myself.

His lips brushed my flesh.

"A touch!" Loki crowed, though I didn't know how he could see from across the campfire.

"It was me," I panted. "An accident." I let my head fall back. My body was a heavy weight, a pendulum—any movement might swing me over into the pleasure I craved. "You gave me one accident."

"Let that be the only one." Loki prowled closer, crouching near so he could catch any more slip ups.

Ragnar groped blindly about him. He found a new, green leaf and brought it to the folds of my sex. I held my breath as he drew it back and forth, tickling my sensitive spots. The sensation was agony, stimulating me without pushing me over the edge. My insides tightened, the coil of need ready to snap.

Minutes passed, and I twisted this way and that, trying to

find relief. The leaf danced over my labia until its green surface shone slick.

"Do you admit defeat?" Loki asked finally.

"No," Ragnar said. "No." But he dropped the leaf and stood.

No... I wanted to howl.

Ragnar scrubbed a hand across his face. When he dropped his hand, his eyes flared bright, torches in the night. He stalked back and stood a little way away, his burly arms crossed over his chest. "But let's see you do better."

Loki slid to my side. "Rosalind," he whispered. His wintergreen scent blew over me, cooling my skin, making me crave his heat. I whimpered. My sex pulsed, craving stimulation. My toes were scrunched in my boots.

He drew down my skirts, then cupped his hand over the fabric, his fingers molding to my cunny underneath. The touch was too much, and not enough. His fingers strummed my sex, the sensation muted by the thick fabric, but still enough to send a fresh wave of arousal through me. I rose to my tiptoes.

"Not fair," I whispered.

"I don't play fair." He dipped his head close until his black hair tickled the rim of my ear.

He leaned back, winding a few locks of his hair into a tight braid. He licked the end of the braid and raised it to my ear, brushing his hair over the sensitive rim, then thrusting the braid inside.

I felt a rush in my sex. I gritted my teeth and fought against it.

"No, don't fight, little runaway. Let yourself go over."

I jerked in my bonds as an invisible brace caught my hips. A tongue-like sensation slid up my inner thigh, licking my lower folds.

What magic is this? I panted, too overcome to ask what was happening. Loki's right eye gleamed green. The other was black as the night sky.

The unseen tongues kept lapping at me. One of them plunged inside.

"Oh," I cried. My fingers dug into the rope, hanging on for dear life.

"Louder," Loki ordered. The tongues at my sex licked harder.

My orgasm bloomed, shaking me in its grip. A cry escaped me before I could stop it.

Ragnar cursed.

"He cheated," I gasped. I jerked in my bonds, but couldn't escape the tickling sensation at my sex. I twisted to face Loki, whose mouth was spread in a wicked grin. "You cheated."

"He didn't touch you," Ragnar said, baring his teeth. "I saw."

I shook my head.

"A kiss." Loki gripped my chin and laid his mouth over mine. "I claim my kiss." His tongue thrust into my mouth.

Then his lips trailed down my neck.

My laces loosened and suddenly my dress and shift hung slack from my shoulders. One tug, and Loki had stripped the garments away. They fell in a pile at my feet. I hung naked, arms above my head. A sacrifice laid bare.

"Yes," Loki said, his lips still locked on my skin, just over my right breast. My nipple prickled in the night air.

"My kiss," he murmured against my skin. "Still the same kiss." His lips never left my flesh as he dragged his mouth lower. His tongue probed my belly button, and my legs locked tight.

"The same kiss." He wrenched my legs apart. I was panting now, my head bowed, my hair spilling over my shoulders. Loki propped one of my legs over his shoulder and planted his mouth at the apex of my sex. I threw my head back, my cries rising like a wolf's howl.

Loki gripped my thighs, keeping his mouth fastened on my cunny, thrusting his tongue inside and drinking my juices like mead.

The sensation of tongues over my flesh increased, and I screamed my climax to the moon. The sensation didn't stop. My climaxes rolled over me again and again, until tears ran down my face. I was lost in a roiling ocean, tossed about by the waves of pleasure. I twisted my wrists in my bonds until drops of liquid fell on my face—sweat or blood, I did not know.

"Rosalind, Rosalind," Ragnar murmured. His large hands stroked my naked back, grounding me. "Easy." He steadied me, cutting the rope above my head and catching me when I would have crumpled to the ground. Gently he bore me down, cradling me in his lap. His thumb rubbed my lax lower lip.

Loki kept his mouth on my sex, lying down with me until he was stretched out between my legs. I was limp in Ragnar's arms.

Only after a final, weak climax did Loki rise up, licking his lips, looking like a cat who'd feasted on cream.

"There," he said smugly to Ragnar. "Now she's too sleepy to run." He rubbed his mouth and tasted his fingers. My body convulsed in pleasure yet again.

I turned my face away. My body still trembled with after-shocks. My core felt raw.

Loki frowned and squatted close to me. His hand closed around my ankle.

"No!" I jerked in his hold, trying to kick free.

"Hush," he soothed. "It's all right. It's over."

"What is wrong?" Ragnar sat up further, propping me

against him with an arm braced around my front. "Did you hurt her?"

"No. But too much pleasure can be worse than not enough. Come." Loki knelt closer and opened his arms. "My touch will fix it. Give her to me."

A growl rumbled deep in Ragnar's chest but he relinquished me to Loki. The dark-haired warrior scooped me up and carried me to the fire, where he settled me on his lap. I squeezed my legs together, whimpering at the memory of the invisible tongues on my sex. What had just happened?

Loki fussed over me, wrapping me in his cloak. His scent blanketed me and despite myself, I burrowed deeper into his chest. "There you are. That's the way." He chuckled. "A little food, a little mead, she'll be fine."

"There is no mead," Ragnar said.

"Check my bag." Loki nodded towards a tree. Ragnar went and found a large sack leaning against it.

"You didn't have a bag before," I whispered.

Loki winked at me. His eyes were back to their normal dual colors. But this time, his left eye was green. Before I could stop myself, I reached up to touch his face.

Loki put a finger to my lips. "Shhh. Did you find the mead?" he asked Ragnar loudly.

Ragnar tossed the small skin in our direction. It landed in the dirt, but within Loki's reach.

"There's fish, too—" Loki added.

"Found it," Ragnar said.

Loki tipped me back so I could drink, while Ragnar grumbled and built up the fire. The honeyed brew renewed me, but when Ragnar had finished cooking the fish, Loki wouldn't let me feed myself. I was still naked, cloaked only by my hair.

"You did well, Rosalind," Loki whispered.

"You cheated," I whispered back. "I don't know how, but you did."

"Shhh." He pushed a bit of baked fish between my lips. "Eat more, love, and regain your strength," he said, louder.

"So, you won." Ragnar poked the fire, glaring at it like it was Loki's face. "Now what?"

"We continue our quest."

"What quest?" Ragnar noticed me shivering and pulled the cloak from Loki's pack. Loki turned me in his lap so Ragnar could wrap me up.

Loki shook his head. "Don't you wonder how one woman got past the Berserker guard? The witches willed it, and so it was." He pointed to my boots. "The witches gave her those. They told her to go on a quest, but she can't speak about it, can she?"

Ragnar looked to me. "Rosalind?"

I licked my lips and shook my head.

"You can't prove it." Ragnar's forehead wrinkled.

"I couldn't… if I were only a man," Loki said.

Ragnar huffed. "This again."

"You know I'm telling the truth." Loki raised his right hand and flicked his fingers. "As it stands, I have a little magic." The air thickened, energy buzzing up my bare arms. A minty scent washed over me, strong as wintergreen berries.

I whimpered.

"Shhh, you're not hurt. Sensitive to magic, are you?" He rubbed my arms and the sensation lessened. "I've created a spell to shield us from the Corpse King's ears. You can speak freely here."

I opened my mouth, and found that I could. The spell stopping my throat was gone. "It's true," I told Ragnar. "The witches gave me a moonstone dagger. They said I must defeat the Corpse King."

"But how?" Ragnar asked in a rough voice. "Not even a Berserker can stand against the mage."

He didn't say it but I heard it all the same: *this quest will be your doom.* I hung my head.

"No." Ragnar crouched before me, cupping my cheek in a rough hand. "I will not let you go."

I leaned into his hand, my eyes closing. His scent surrounded me.

"Touching," Loki said. "But she must go. She is our only hope." He shifted me onto Ragnar's lap and pulled my feet into his. His thumbs dug into my arches, rubbing in the most delicious way. My eyelids fluttered.

"What am I to do? I have to complete this quest. You don't understand—"

"Try and explain." Loki rubbed my heels.

I made myself speak clearly. "I must atone. It's my fault the Corpse King nearly came to possess the moonstone in the first place."

"But you were carrying it to the heart of his power," Ragnar pointed out, tugging on his beard.

"In my hands, it is a weapon against him—"

Ragnar dropped his hand and slapped the ground. "But do you know how to use it?"

I buried my face in my hands.

"Enough," Loki said. "She's tired. We are safe here. She can rest, and we can keep watch."

Together, the warriors laid me between them. Ragnar gathered my wrists and bound them in front of me.

"She's too tired to run," Loki protested. I did not hear Ragnar's answer because I had already surrendered into sleep.

CHAPTER 6

osalind

WHEN I AWOKE, the sun was already slanting through the trees.

I pushed myself up, feeling stiff. Ragnar crouched near me, loosening the bindings around my wrists.

I found my tongue. "You let me sleep."

His eyes crinkled as he touched my hair. "You needed it."

I licked my lips, enjoying his touch. We were newfound allies, but Ragnar was still dangerous. And distraction from my quest was dangerous.

"Where is Loki?"

The warmth in Ragnar's face faded. "Gone to scout ahead." He reached behind him and lifted a dark bundle of fabric. He shook it out, and I gasped. The bundle unfurled in a rich waterfall of shimmering purple, so dark it was almost black. It was a gown such as I'd never seen. A gown fit for a queen.

"Loki left you this." Ragnar pushed the bundle into my hands as if he resented it.

I touched the shining brocade. "Magic made this."

He grunted.

"Ragnar, who is Loki? Do you know him?"

"I thought I did. I remember him as a warrior. But he claims he's a god."

Loki's perfect face flashed in my mind. "Could it be true?"

"If it is, let us hope he's really on our side." He started to rise, and I stopped him with a hand on his arm.

"Do you trust him?"

"Not a bit," he answered, and sighed. "Rosalind," he took my hands in his, rubbing his thumbs over my wrists to smooth the marks the bindings had left, "if it is true what you both say about the witches choosing you for this quest, then I wronged you by trying to bring you back."

"It's all right. I understand." I bowed my head, hoping to hide the flush his touch brought to my cheeks.

His eyes flashed gold. "What I cannot make out is why they would send you, so young and untested, to face this monster."

I tugged my hands away, burying them in the folds of my new gown. I didn't like to speak of this. I wished for a moment that the geis was on me again. "I told you. I have the Corpse King's mark on me." My fingers twitched, wanting to scrub at my own forehead. It wouldn't help. The mark wasn't something that could be washed away. Back on Berserker Mountain, I'd tried all manner of soap and scrubbing. All winter, I'd tried. And the Corpse King's whispers had stolen into my sleep. It was enough to drive a woman mad. No wonder I had agreed to the quest. It was the only way to free my mind.

A deep growl burst from Ragnar's chest, startling us both.

"Is there no way to remove it?" His voice dripped with the guttural tones of the beast.

"The witches said they would send helpers to guide me." I tucked my knees under my chin. Should I tell him the next part? "You kissed my forehead back when we were beset by the army, and my head cleared."

Ragnar remained silent, but his whole body was rigid with the stillness of a predator. I laid a hand on his taut forearm, my thumb stroking over the veins roping the hard muscle. "Long has the Corpse King been linked to my mind. But I think your kiss... did something." There, I'd said it. Now Ragnar knew everything about me.

He dropped his head close enough for his braids to brush mine. "Do you think that did it?" he purred. His arm came around me, drawing me close.

"I don't know." I leaned into him. "Something happened. It... helped."

"Perhaps we should do it again." His breath tickled my ear. He ducked his head, nuzzling my cheek. "Just to be sure."

"Ragnar—" Any protest I had, died. I closed my eyes and tilted my face up to his, offering my mouth.

This time, his kiss was gentle. His lips played over mine, brushing, teasing. Seducing. Rough fingers caught my chin, holding me still for a deeper kiss. His tongue slipped into my mouth. The gentle probing turned to plunder.

Heat flooded my body like I'd sipped fine mead, honey simmering in my veins. I turned in Ragnar's embrace, facing him more fully. The gown slipped off my lap. I didn't care. My body buzzed, my bare skin wanting to press against his.

Someone in the distance cleared their throat. I was too far away to care.

"As much as I love this," Loki's mocking voice cut into the haze, "it's time to go."

A shadow cut across us. Loki stood over us, his arms

folded across his chest, an assessing look on his narrow face. I jerked in Ragnar's arms, but he did not let me go.

"You are interrupting," Ragnar muttered, still nuzzling along my neck. I snatched the violet gown from where it had spilled to the ground, and used it to shield my naked form.

Loki smirked at me. "It can't be helped. The way is clear. We should be off. There are more undead coming."

Ragnar released me, and I scrambled to my feet. "Give me a moment to get dressed."

As the sun rose, we trekked along, heading deeper into the Corpse King's lands.

Loki went ahead, scouting, his black-clad form slipping through the trees. Ragnar stuck to my side, a walking monolith shielding my back. His presence calmed me, just as it had before when we were among the draugr, and the Corpse King tried to seize my mind.

I mopped my brow. My boots and dress were too heavy for the heat. My hair was a wretched mess, soaked with sweat, dirty from my nights sleeping on the ground. I used to be such a vain girl but now I would do whatever it took to go where I must and complete the quest.

"All clear ahead." Loki rejoined us, sounding cheerful. He swung into step on my right side. His dark hair was neat and shining like a raven's wing, his black clothes immaculate. I envied and hated him at the same time. Maybe it was his rich, well-fitting garb, or maybe it was his two-toned eyes, but something about Loki unsettled me. There was a touch of unworldliness about him, as if he really was a familiar the witches had summoned to help me. A familiar who happened to be in the shape of a man.

Loki certainly was beautiful. A more perfectly formed face I'd never seen. Ragnar was brutally handsome, with rough-hewn features and a broken nose. He looked exactly as he was—a warrior, a marauder sent to kill and plunder his way through the Earth. Loki looked like a prince, or a proud member of the elven race who was only visiting human lands. There was an elegance to his walk, as if the air around him smoothed his way. I found myself walking close to him, as if he were a lodestone and I was a nail. His long, elegant fingers kept drawing my eye, bringing back the memory of the magic they'd wrought on my flesh, even though it would do me no good to lust after such a man.

My stupid body didn't heed the warning. Stuck walking between the two, my skin prickled with awareness. Was it only last night they strung me up between them and had a contest over who could first bring me to climax?

My boot caught a stone and I pitched forward.

"Careful," Loki said, putting out a hand, but Ragnar actually caught me with a hand on my elbow. I regained my footing but Ragnar kept hold of me.

"We need to rest," the blond warrior grunted.

"No," I said. "I'm fine." I tucked a sweaty tendril of my hair behind my ear. "We need to keep going."

"So eager she is to rush to our doom." Loki's voice was mocking but his eyes held a certain knowledge. I shook my head at him when Ragnar wasn't looking at me.

"Why do you say that?" Ragnar demanded. Now his hand was on my shoulder, tucking me into his side.

Loki shrugged. "This mission is madness. No one knows that more than Rosalind. But I am here to assist in any way." He bowed at the waist.

"Madman," Ragnar muttered, and swung me to face him. "Rosalind, we do not have to go on."

"No," I said. "I must."

After a pause, Ragnar nodded as if it was his choice and not mine. His protectiveness annoyed and thrilled me.

I was so perverse. Of all the men in the world, I desired one who was always at odds with me, and another who had strange magic and thought he was a god. Both were dangerous monsters in their own way.

The further into the forest we went, the more oppressive the humidity grew. The silence.

"Strange," I said, more to break the silence than anything.

"What is strange?" Loki asked. Ragnar held a branch aside for me to scuttle past.

"I was thinking." I said. "When I was a child at the orphanage, I was told never to wander into the forest. The nuns scared us with stories of beasts and frightening things that would carry us off."

"How right they were," Loki said, raising a brow in Ragnar's direction.

I shook my head. "Then I grew older and learned the real monsters are not beasts lurking in the forest, but men. It's a wonder I'd not braved the forest before." It would have been preferable to my life in the abbey. Maybe I could have escaped before I'd become broken.

"There is nothing to fear," Ragnar said after a pause. "We will protect you."

"Rosalind speaks of horrors long ago endured," Loki said. I didn't like how he seemed to read my mind.

I squinted at him. "Perhaps you should scout ahead."

"Perhaps." There was an amused tilt to his eyes. He was mocking me.

"Shall we take turns?" he said to Ragnar. "You stay by her side, and I'll scout. Then we switch. I'll go first." Loki strode ahead before Ragnar could disagree or agree.

Ragnar grimaced and shook his head. "I do not trust him."

"Let me know if he tries to kiss you again. I'll protect you." I patted his arm.

We marched in silence. Ragnar hovered by my side, his large hands gripping the handle of his axe, his head constantly swiveling back and forth to search for danger.

Every once in a while, he sniffed the wind. He would scent the Corpse King's armies before we saw them.

My foot caught the edge of a log, and Ragnar caught my elbow and steadied me before I stumbled. "How's your ankle?"

"It's fine." I gave him a nod.

He rubbed a hand over his face and swept a hand out, indicating I should lead the way. I felt the heat of his stare on my back. If I were to look into his mind, I would see his singlemost desire: to carry me back to safety. I pushed my way through a thick maze of branches, waiting for his frustration to break and his questions to come.

Finally, they did. "Rosalind, why did the witches choose you?"

"I don't know," I said, although I did. I hated to speak of my secret shame, the affinity I had for the Corpse King. I'd already told Ragnar of the mark I bore. Did I have to explain again?

"And what's the plan? How are you meant to end this quest?"

I grimaced and looked to Loki. *Help me.*

"The witches warned her not to speak of the plan," Loki told Ragnar. "They were afraid it would attract the mage's attention. They put a geis upon her, a spell to block her voice. But here, we are safe. Try, Rosalind."

I opened my mouth and waited for the witch's spell to block my answer but nothing happened. So I could tell him. "There's a weapon—the dagger. I am supposed to use it on him. The moonstone is his weakness. The witches will be able to destroy him through it. My part is small. But I am the witch's best chance of getting close."

"Because you bear his mark," Ragnar muttered and I nodded, my cheeks burning. I was ashamed. Of all the spaewives, I was the one marked by the Corpse King. It must have been my fault. I had drawn him to me somehow, without meaning to. And then I had been too weak to resist his hold. All winter, I'd lived with the guilt.

Perhaps it would be a good thing if I did not survive this quest.

"Once you have attacked him, then what?" Ragnar asked as if he could sense the thread of my thoughts.

I shrugged.

A growl tore through him. He grabbed my arm, forcing me to stop. "Show me, then," he said. "Show me how you use this weapon."

I clutched at the front of my gown, pressing the dagger into my chest. "What?"

"Let us practice." Ragnar gestured impatiently. I half-turned from him to draw the dagger out from its hidden place between my breasts. A milky blue light flooded my face.

"No," he said before I could lift the thong over my head. "Best keep that hidden."

I agreed and hid the dagger again.

"Here," he handed me one of his daggers, "let us practice. That is the Corpse King." He pointed to a tree. "Let me see your grip."

I showed him how I held the dagger. He rearranged my fingers so the hilt lay more easily in my palm. "Yes." His big hand closed over mine.

"Now, thrust. Underhand, like this." He drew my entire arm forward in a smooth, sudden motion. I closed my eyes and tried to imagine the dagger sliding between a man's ribs.

"Again." He repeated the movement several times until I was faster. "Now…" He turned me so I was facing the tree. His hands on my shoulders steadied me. "Drive it into the trunk."

I tried, but my unsteady movement barely drove the blade's tip into the bark.

"Lower," he said. "You need all your weight behind it." He had me hold the dagger right at my hip so I could snap my arm forward and lean into the strike. My first attempt chipped away a chunk of bark. He helped me tug the dagger free and try again with his big body at my back. Together, we practiced a smoother strike.

"That's the way," he murmured right into my ear. "Try again."

I thrust the dagger forward using the strength of my hips.

"Good," Ragnar murmured. His body leaned into mine. I jerked the dagger out of the tree and slammed into his hard chest. His hands came to my hips, holding me close. A weapon prodded my bottom—not his axe or dagger, but his cock.

"Is this a two-person game?" Loki's mocking voice rang out behind us. "Or can I play?" The dark haired warrior ambled into view.

"Go away," Ragnar said.

Loki ignored him and came to slouch against the tree we were attacking. "What did this tree do that you would stab it so?"

"Are you volunteering to take its place?" Ragnar pivoted me so Loki was in reach. "Hold still. It's for a good cause."

"Ragnar," I protested.

"Oh no." Loki stepped forward, pulling down the collar of his jerkin to bare the smooth skin over his heart. "Strike true, dear Rosalind."

"It's no use." I dropped my arm, letting the dagger point to the ground. "I cannot strike the Corpse King's heart."

"I would not be so sure of that." Loki came forward and took up my arm. "The moonstone has a mind of its own." He drew my arm forward so the dagger touched his chest. My eyes met his, and my insides shifted. For a moment, it seemed as if I could hear his heartbeat and match mine to his.

"Do you feel it, dear Rosalind?" Loki murmured.

"Enough." Ragnar pulled me back and the spell was broken.

I shook my head to clear it. Ragnar glared at Loki. Any moment, the two warriors would have weapons at each other's throats.

"Let's walk on." I cleared my throat.

"What a lovely idea," Loki said. "Brother, it's your turn to scout ahead."

"Not your brother," Ragnar grumbled.

"Don't worry," Loki purred. "I will take good care of Rosalind." His look made me bite my lip. Was it wise to be alone with him? Something about the strange warrior drew me, almost as if there was some magic to him. It made me wary. I already had a connection to one mage, I didn't need another.

Ragnar stood, gripping his axe, looking at Loki like he'd need no reason to cleave the dark hair from his neck.

"Go," I told Ragnar. "I will be all right."

With a frown, the blond Berserker stomped into the wood.

Loki rubbed his hands together. "Now that he's gone, shall we have a practice session of our own?"

"Should we not keep walking?" I lifted my skirts and strode ahead, following Ragnar's trail.

Loki strolled along behind me. I felt his gaze on my back.

"Are you coming?" I snapped.

He cocked his head to the side. "I prefer the view from here."

"Oh, you foolish man." I marched back and took his arm.

"Ah now, this is nice." He settled his hand on top of mine

as if we were lovers ambling to a trysting spot. I hid the thrill his touch gave me. "A fine day for a stroll through the forest."

"Until we encounter the draugr," I countered.

"I doubt we will see them any time soon."

"Because we have passed them?"

Loki shrugged. "Or the Corpse King feels you are coming closer, and he desires to draw you near. He will only send his servants if you turn and run the opposite way."

"How do you know this?"

His mouth curved in a mirthless smile. "I know things."

I dropped his arm and put some distance between us. "Ragnar says you think you are a god."

He spread his hands wide. "Aren't I god-like?"

I rubbed my forehead. "You make me want to throw things."

"Freya says the same thing." He bowed and extended his hand. "Especially when I do this." The moonstone shone in his palm.

I clutched the leather noose around my neck. The dagger was there but the moonstone was gone. "Loki!"

"Calm yourself." The moonstone danced over his fingers like it had last time, disappearing between each knuckle only to pop up between the next.

Despite myself, I took a step forward. It was mesmerizing. After a minute watching, I finally murmured, "You need to give it back."

"Mmm, perhaps I will. Perhaps I won't."

I sighed. "What do you want for it?"

"How well you know me. Yes, let us bargain." Loki threw the moonstone in the air and caught it, then showed me his empty palm. He'd made the stone disappear.

I swallowed my scream of frustration.

"Tell me this, Rosalind," Loki's half grin mocked me, "you

are young, with no skills and no magic. Yet the witches chose you of all people to carry out this quest."

"Yes. I know." My voice was curt. What was he asking?

He tilted his head, less mocking, more curious. "Why are you doing this?"

"Why are you?" I shot back.

He shrugged. "Once I finish this favor, the witches will petition Odinn for my powers back. Your turn. And no lies."

I swallowed. "For my sister. So she can have a good life."

Loki stepped close. Shadows slanted across his high cheekbones. The whole of his attention was on me, and I felt he could see down to my bones. "What about you?" He tucked a sweat-soaked strand of my hair behind my ear. "Do you not desire to have a good life?"

"It's too late for me. But not for her."

"Hmmm." Loki tapped his mouth with his long, elegant fingers as he studied me. "I simply don't understand what you have to gain. You know as well as I do that you won't—"

I cut him off before he could say more. "Have you ever done something for anyone other than yourself?"

He pursed his lips as if thinking carefully. "No."

I scoffed. "At least you're honest."

"I don't want to be a hero. I would settle for not being a villain." He opened his hand and the moonstone was back in his palm. As I watched, he threaded it nimbly though his fingers again.

I went to grab it and he held it aloft.

The frustration boiling in my breast bubbled over. "Is this a game to you? Because it isn't to me."

He held up his hands. "For the first time in my long existence, I am mortal. I am used to playing games, passing the time with tricks. But now life is no game. Excuse me while I adjust to that."

"Well, you're going to have to adjust faster," I snapped.

"This quest means life and death for me. If you are too selfish to understand that, then leave. Your help isn't wanted."

I whirled and marched through the trees.

"Rosalind," Loki called, and when I didn't turn, he strode after me. I ducked away, pushing through a cluster of towering pine. Their needled branches whipped my face. I didn't care.

"Odinn's beard, Rosalind, stop."

Long as his legs were, Loki caught up with me. He pulled me from the snarl of branches. I held still, my face frozen in stubborn hurt as he pulled pine needles from my hair.

"Little runaway, I'm sorry."

"You're supposed to help me."

"I am. Here." He took my hand and put the moonstone in my palm.

"It's useless like this. It's supposed to stay on the dagger—"

"No. Indulge me a moment." He lifted my hand. "Can you slip it through your fingers, as I did?"

I closed my hand around the gem and clutched it to my chest. "Why?" I wrinkled my nose at him.

"I want to test something. Just try, Rosalind. For me."

Sullenly, I held out my hand. My fingers and thumb moved of their own volition, rolling the moonstone over my knuckles.

He rocked back on his heels, looking smug. "As I thought."

"What?" I demanded.

"You have an... affinity."

"An affinity," I repeated flatly.

"Magic, Rosalind. You have magic."

I sputtered, and he held up a hand.

"Your power is untrained, untested. The witches didn't have time to teach you. Don't worry. When the time comes, you will know what to do."

I gripped the moonstone again in my palm. Was it my mind, or did the gem pulse with a faint magical energy? "I don't understand."

"Show me the trick again." He waited patiently as I regarded him.

This time, I thought too hard. I fumbled the stone a few times, but was still able to maneuver it properly over my knuckles once or twice.

"You're a natural," Loki murmured at my shoulder. He stood with his head bowed over mine, close enough to make my skin prickle.

I drew back from him, heading to a log to sit. "The stone should be on the dagger." I pulled out the dagger and fitted the moonstone onto the pommel, fixing the silver strands of wire so they held the stone in place.

I did not ask how Loki had conjured it to his hand, but he read my questioning look.

"It has a mind of its own." Loki shrugged, which was not a real answer. "Like it's owner."

"It's not mine. The witches gave it to me." I bit my lip, afraid to ask more. "You said I have an affinity... what did you mean?"

He shrugged. "I don't know for certain, but it seems you quickly attune to the magic around you. Absorb it. An interesting skill that may be useful on this quest—but why do you look like that? Rosalind, what is wrong?"

Despair had risen up and clogged my throat. "You were right. The witches were foolish to choose me for this quest."

He seated himself on the log next to me, his face sober. "Why do you say that?"

"The Corpse King knows I am susceptible to magic. He has used me as his pawn." I rubbed my eyes. "My affinity is not a skill. It is a weakness. I am not an ally. I am one of the enemy. If I am to be the world's salvation, I fear the quest was over before it began. I am sentencing everyone to doom."

Loki gathered me into his lap before I could protest. "Rosalind," he said gently. "It is said the Corpse King can reach into minds and make them despair. He can make men fear him and drive them mad. That is how he amasses his armies of undead. But he can affect the living too." He threaded a hand into my hair. "You have been under this melancholy for some time. Since before the Corpse King sought you out."

There was an invisible fist around my throat, squeezing. But still I got the answer out. "Yes."

A slow nod. The look in Loki's eye was almost tender. "How long has it plagued you?"

"Since I was left at the orphanage." I pressed my lips together because I didn't want to talk about this anymore. I pushed myself from his lap and straightened my gown. By the time I was done, Loki's mask was back in place. A cynical smile was slanted over his strangely beautiful face.

"An orphan who holds the fate of the world in her hands. It will be a marvelous story."

"Will you tell it?" I kept my voice brisk.

"I will. If I live." He stood and rubbed his hand against his breeches. "Now, remember the trick. It is a better skill than learning to use a dagger."

"Trickery?" Of course he would say that.

Loki pointed to the front of my gown, right at the moonstone hidden under the layers of fabric and the leather sheath. "That stone is our salvation. Not the dagger. The stone is how you will beat the Corpse King." He saw my expression and touched my cheek. "Cheer up. He will not suspect you."

"I fear I am bound to fail," I whispered.

His thumb stroked down my jaw. "Don't say that. If you die, I die with you."

I pushed at his hand. "We will all die if I fail."

"Then I will use all my tricks to help you succeed." He faced me full on, cupping my face in his hands. I gazed up at him—he was taller than Ragnar, taller than anyone I'd ever met. And so beautiful.

"I will teach you." He stared at my mouth. My lips prickled with readiness. "You have many weapons, Rosalind, not just the dagger." His face was so close, our breath mingled. "Bedazzle your enemy." His green eye glinted.

A surge of arousal pushed me to my tiptoes. I brushed my lips against his. Energy shot between us, crackling like lightning. My skin buzzed.

I gripped the front of his jerkin, dragging him closer. I pressed my mouth to his, harder, soothing the frantic need in my breast.

Loki laughed even as his mouth met mine. "That's it, that's the way."

"This is fighting?" I murmured against his lips.

"Yes. You fight so well." His chest was heaving under my palm, and I knew he felt what I felt. A warm touch moved up my back, a hot, liquid hand. Loki's real hands were gripping my arms so this touch could only be magic.

It felt so good. I leaned into it a little, letting the sensation spread across my skin. Soon, my entire back was covered with the soothing warmth, and I silently begged the fluid feeling to move downward.

"You want power, Rosalind?"

I jerked back because I had told Ragnar I wanted power. But not Loki. Was this more evidence that Loki could read minds?

"You have power. Great power." His hand slipped down my bodice to cup my sex. "You need only to own it." The magical warmth spread downwards, gliding over my buttocks, dripping down my thighs.

Fire fizzed in my bloodstream. I lifted my leg and Loki caught it, hooking it around his hip so I could grind my cunny against him. He bent over me, his lips and tongue hungry on mine, plundering. My breasts swelled until my gown was too tight. I clawed at Loki's jerkin as if I could tear the leather like parchment. I was a beast. I was hungry for his skin, for his lips and tongue, for his heavy weight pinning my body to the forest floor and his cock pumping his cum into me.

"Rosalind." Loki caught my frantic wrists. "Easy. Rosalind."

I was growling like a Berserker. I was mad.

"Rosalind…" A voice echoed through the trees, bringing me back to myself. Calling my attention back to somber reality and the nature of my quest. Must I be simply a vessel for the Corpse King's doom? Couldn't I take one moment to be myself?

"Rosalind." It was Ragnar, calling my name.

I pushed Loki away and stepped back to straighten my gown before Ragnar came through the trees. I didn't want him to see me pressing against Loki. It felt like a betrayal.

How had my heart gotten so entangled? I had never wanted any man, now I craved two. Two who hated each other. And it didn't matter, anyway. Everything I had, all my love and devotion, must be sacrificed to the quest.

Ragnar appeared and made his way to me.

Loki stepped in front of me, stopping him short. The move both annoyed Ragnar, and gave me a moment to collect myself. Knowing Loki, he meant his actions to have two results.

"What have you found?" Loki asked.

"Nothing for miles ahead. But the wind carries the thick stench of draugr. We may be walking into a trap."

"No." Loki sounded bored. "We're walking into the heart of the Corpse King's power. We are very near it, if not *in* it. We must be wary. We will stumble upon his lair soon." He looked straight at me with his mismatched eyes. "If not today, then tomorrow."

I opened my mouth, then closed it. I had nothing to say. What could I do? Wishing for more time with these warriors would not give it to me. "Let's be off then." I strode into the forest with my head held high.

One more night. I had one more night with the Berserkers. Then I would confront the Corpse King in his lair.

One way or another, my quest would end.

* * *

A LOW LEVEL of clouds blanketed the sky. I trudged with my head down. Each step seemed to be uphill. Ragnar led the way, threading through boulders and sharp rocks that threatened to slice through our boots.

"Here," he said and I raised my head. We were on a hill, overlooking a long plain covered in a grey mist that matched the low-lying clouds above. In the distance, there was some movement.

"Draugr," Ragnar snarled. He pointed to the teeming mass. "There. And there."

"So many."

It was just like the dream I'd had, except instead of the Corpse King, I had Ragnar and Loki at my side.

The Corpse King's army was a silvery sea.

I should recoil and run the opposite way but I felt nothing. My heart was empty. I had felt everything there was to feel, and now that my quest was almost done, there was nothing more for me but to go on.

"Another few miles of walking, and we will be upon them," Ragnar grunted.

"We can sneak around them," Loki said.

"And then what?" Ragnar ran a hand over his braids. "What is the plan?"

"We walk in together," I said. "The witches said I must not be separated from my helpers." I looked into Loki's eyes as I spoke. He nodded slowly. He knew what I was saying. Only he had been sent to help me. Ragnar must be left behind. He would not thank me, but it would save his life.

The air had an opaque quality to it.

"What is this strange fog?" Ragnar croaked.

"It's smoke," I choked out. "They are burning funeral pyres."

"The Corpse King gains power from sacrifice," Loki said, and we fell silent after that.

I kept my head down. My steps grew slow, as if I were dragging my boots through mud.

Tomorrow, I would walk into the Corpse King's lair. Alone. All alone.

There would never be any hope for me again.

The mist rose around me, thicker than smoke. My limbs moved slowly, as if I was in water.

Too late, the mist cleared and revealed the briars tearing at my gown. Thorns wide as my fingers pierced my skirts and scratched my skin. I felt nothing, but when I thrashed, I couldn't move. I was trapped.

"Rosalind." I heard Ragnar's voice, frantic. "Rosalind, come back to me!"

He touched me, and I was able to breathe again. His scent was clean, a relief after the burning mouthfuls of foul air. His palm patted my face.

"Gentle," Loki cautioned.

"She's rousing." Ragnar held me as I coughed. Ash burned in my lungs.

Loki's long fingers stroked my face. "Let's get to shelter."

"Can you clear the air of this wretched smoke?" Ragnar snapped.

"I can try." For once, Loki was grim, not joking.

I pressed my face against Ragnar's shoulder, breathing in his dry cedar scent. It cut through the mist in my head. "I'm fine."

"Hush now." Loki pressed three fingers to my forehead, right at the spot where the Corpse King had marked me. Where Ragnar had kissed me, and I still felt the brush of his lips. "Close your eyes and rest."

* * *

MAYBE IT WAS the weight of the mage's magic. Maybe it was Loki's touch. But when I closed my eyes, I dreamed of them both.

First, the memory of the Corpse King, his eyes burning like moonstones. I was lost, and blundered through the forest, dragging my sister along behind me. I thought I saw a light ahead, through the black tree trunks. I thought perhaps it was a fire, some sort of rescue. But when I drew near, it was only a cloaked figure clad in mist. The flicker of light was gone.

And then the mage turned and fixed me with his burning eyes.

"Aspen, run," I tried to tell her, but she shook her small head and would not go. I wouldn't want us to be separated, either. We'd been together since the villagers had left us outside the orphanage.

So I tucked her behind me as best I could. She would not let go of my hand.

"Who are you?" I asked.

"Close... closer," he said.

I struggled. His voice trapped me. It was deep and seemed to echo, like it came from the bottom of a well. I took one step and another, my sister's small hand in mine. She came along, trusting me to keep her safe.

Somehow, I forced my legs to stop a few feet away from the specter. In the forest behind us there were shouts and roars, sounds of battle. The Berserkers fighting. Some of them dying. As powerful as they were, they could not fight mist and magic. I learned later some of them had gone mad, and forced their brothers to cut them down.

Who was I to stand against the Corpse King? I never had a chance.

"Come to me, my bride."

"No," I said, but it was too late. He'd trapped me. He reached out his hand, and his arm was long enough. His bony finger brushed my forehead.

His image dissolved like mist, but it was too late. From miles away, the Corpse King had sent his apparition to hunt the world for one who would do his bidding. And he had marked me.

"He's in your head, you know," Loki said.

I turned around and the dark forest, the Corpse King, and my sister, all disappeared.

In the second part of my dream, day had returned. But the light was shrouded with mist and clouds. A clean mist that smelled like wintergreen, and not the stench of the draugr.

Loki sat cross legged, eyes closed. His dark hair floated as if in the wind, but if there was a breeze I could not feel it. A moonstone hung from a silver earring in his right ear. His eyes were closed but as I approached, he opened one. The black one.

"I know." I touched my head. "I would kick him out if I could."

"I could try to pry him out of you, but my powers are not what they once were."

I smiled at that. Loki, still going on about being a god. "Perhaps you will regain them."

"Perhaps."

The mist grew thicker now, four white walls closing us in.

"A spell," Loki answered my unasked question. "Keeping us safe."

A roaring sound shook the forest. The mist swirled but whatever monster prowled just outside the glade, it could not get in.

"He wants you." Whether he meant Ragnar or the Corpse King, I did not know. Perhaps he meant both.

I touched the wall of mist. It was sturdy as a rock.

"It's not to be," I whispered to the monster beyond the mist.

"A shame," Loki called. Now he was using a stick to write on the ground, his head bent so I couldn't see his eyes. I had the feeling they were both black.

I settled on the ground near Loki. The mist swirled around his hips, so it looked like he was sitting on a cushion of clouds. "You know the truth then," I said.

"The witches told me." His jaw was taut. Runes appeared in the soil, glittering blue before burning away. The smoke joined the wall of mist. "I can't stop it."

"It's all right," I said, and for the first time since I'd accepted my quest, it was. I felt at peace.

CHAPTER 7

WHEN I AWOKE, the air was clear on my face. I was wrapped in a soft cloak that smelled like both Loki and Ragnar— wintergreen, and cedar. I turned my head and found that there were two cloaks, one under me, one over me. I lay between them, surrounded by the scent of both warriors, a delicious blend I wanted to bathe in.

The warriors' voices rose and fell in soothing murmurs close by.

"There must be a way…" Ragnar was muttering.

"There is none." Loki sounded as resigned as he had in my dream. "Do you think I would not have tried it? If I had my powers, I could try something, but—"

"Oh, because you're a god," Ragnar scoffed.

"—but I can do nothing until my full powers are returned."

"So get them back," Ragnar growled.

"It's not that easy. I must complete a quest. I must sacrifice myself for another."

A pause. "But if you die…"

"I die forever, yes. I think they want me to face consequences. They want it to hurt."

Ragnar chuckled. "Welcome to life."

"It's not funny," Loki muttered. He was crouched on the ground near me, writing runes in the dirt. Ash smudged his cheek, and his hair hung lank in his face. He looked less godlike. More human.

Ragnar stopped laughing. "No, it's not."

I shifted a little, and Ragnar's head snapped to mine.

"Rosalind." He rose to crouch by me and brush his fingers over my cheek. "You're awake. Are you cold? We can build a fire." He tucked the edge of the cloak around me and a strong whiff of cedar puffed across my face.

"No fire." I rubbed my eyes. The air around us was clear but a few feet away, a wall of mist rose. We were boxed in by the mist, much like we had been in my dream. I raised my hand towards the night sky—clear but for a few clouds that might have been tendrils of the Corpse King's mist trying to break into our sanctuary.

"Loki did it," Ragnar answered my unspoken question. "He wove a spell around us."

"We are safe for this night," Loki said. "My magic will hold the barrier until morning. No one can penetrate this place."

"And there's food." Ragnar picked up a sack and rummaged in it.

"I'm not hungry," I told them. "I wish to stay here tonight and then in the morning, we go on."

Loki rubbed his face, which spread the charcoal smudge further down his cheek. "Ragnar hopes he can dissuade you from the journey."

I shook my head slowly. "It's my choice. My quest." I met Loki's eyes, and knew he was the same Loki in my dream. And that meant he knew how the quest would end for me.

This quest would be my death. I could not hope to stand against the Corpse King and win. I could only hope to weaken him enough for the witches' attack.

But I still had tonight. And for the first time in a long time, I wanted more than a quick end. For the first time in my life, I wanted a man. Two men. These men. Loki and Ragnar.

I had one night with them. One night, my last night on Earth alive. And I wanted them.

"If we are staying here tonight, I will build a fire," Loki said.

I raised my head. "Is there fresh water?"

"A stream nearby," Ragnar said. He helped me rise, his hands hovering close in case I fell. My footing was firm. I had a plan, and an end goal.

When Ragnar would follow me all the way to the stream, I halted and looked up at him through my lashes. "Might I go alone?"

He looked suspicious.

"I'll be safe," I said, gathering my hair and pulling it over one shoulder so I could finger comb through the tangles. "I promise."

"You promised me that before." His voice was gruff but had a teasing edge.

I smiled and let my hips sway as I walked away.

"Watch her," Loki called from his place by the fire. Ragnar rumbled an answer but I didn't hear it because his back was turned to me.

I walked a little way until the stream curved and the lower ground created a deeper pool. There, I could hide behind the grasses. If I peeped around a birch, I could see

Ragnar's upper half. He was still facing away from the stream, to give me privacy.

I stepped behind a tussock of bog grass and bent to splash water on my face. It was cold and good. I gathered up my skirts to wade into the water. The fresh water on my skin renewed my spirits. So did my plan.

I would seduce Ragnar and Loki. And I knew just how to do it.

Tugging off my boots, I tossed them aside. Then my gown and chemise, and all the layers of underclothes. I waded naked into the deepest part of the pool. A few feet beyond, the water ran into a wall of mist—much like the one in my dream. There was a clear boundary between the clear air and the smoke in front of me—where Loki's spell ended, and the Corpse King's lands began. I waded up to it and touched the barrier. It tingled as my hand passed through.

"Rosalind!" Ragnar splashed into the stream with Loki striding behind. "Were you leaving?" The blond warrior pulled me back from the boundary, searching my eyes as if he expected me to be in a trance, under the Corpse King spell. "Are you with us?"

"Yes," I said. "I am under my own power."

"You would leave us?" Ragnar growled.

"I told you to keep an eye on her." Loki smirked. The strain had fallen from his beautiful face as he beheld my naked form. "How could you fail at such a lovely chore?" His black eyebrows bounced. "Naughty girl."

A laugh bubbled out of me.

"You think this is funny?" Ragnar hoisted me up and tossed me over his shoulder to wade back to the campsite. He'd spread his cloak on the ground in preparation for us to sleep, and here he laid me down, taking care that I did not bang my head on the ground.

I relaxed on my back, still laughing.

Ragnar frowned down at me. "You said you would not run. You promised."

"I've made promises before." I smiled at him. My cheeks felt strange. It wasn't often they curved with mirth.

"We agreed that we would go together."

"I changed my mind. Perhaps you should punish me," I taunted.

Twin fires flared in Ragnar's eyes. "Do not toy with me—"

"Brother," Loki interrupted. "Perhaps we should punish her. I think she deserves a little chastisement, don't you?"

Ragnar did not protest that Loki called him *brother*. "Perhaps you are right." He pulled me up and dragged me to a low, wide rock, where he sat down. In one move, he pulled me up and settled me over his lap.

"She's already naked," Loki observed. "Convenient."

"Perhaps we should keep her this way," Ragnar's voice rumbled through me. His rough hand slid up the back of my bare leg. "Naked. Bound. At our mercy."

"Her bottom could use more pink." Loki circled around the rock, studying me from different angles.

I squirmed on Ragnar's hard thighs. I hated how they spoke about me like I wasn't there.

Ragnar slapped my bottom. "Be still."

"Again," Loki said. Ragnar obliged, spanking my right rear cheek until the flesh burned.

"Very nice."

I was ready with a sharp comment, but when I opened my mouth, Loki crouched in front of me and shoved two fingers between my lips.

"Hush now," he said in that patronizing lord-of-all-he-surveyed manner. "We have no use for this at present."

I glared at him.

"I think she likes having her mouth filled," Loki remarked to Ragnar.

I cursed, and Loki's fingers pressed on my tongue. Fluid burst from my core in response.

Loki cocked his head and sniffed the air. "And my, my, what a sweet scent."

"Her cunny needs tending." Ragnar slid his hand over my bottom... and lower, until his fingers brushed my sensitive nether lips. "But she doesn't deserve it. Not yet."

"Better make her earn it," Loki agreed.

Ragnar took his hand away from my needy center and squeezed my rear cheeks, warming them up.

"I could find some wild ginger and whittle it into a plug to heat her insides," Loki mused. "She would burn within, and without."

"Next time," Ragnar grunted. The log of his cock pressed into my belly. "Let's turn these cheeks red."

He spanked me hard enough to make me lurch forward and half swallow Loki's fingers.

"Easy." Loki removed his fingers and steadied my shoulders.

Ragnar's hand rose and fell in a steady rhythm. His palm caught the full breadth of my cheeks with a harsh tattoo of slaps.

Loki bent down to brush his lips over my face. "I claim another kiss," he said.

I averted my head. I knew about his kisses. They were dangerous.

"The most dangerous weapon," Loki agreed as if I'd spoken out loud. His long fingers caressed my face. Ragnar's palm caught the underside of my bottom, making me gasp. As my lips parted, Loki tilted his head and fitted his mouth to mine. The touch of his lips pulled me onto a new plane of arousal. Heat rose around me, the pain in my bottom distant as Loki drank of me. His tongue swept into my mouth, stroking the insides of my cheeks as if searching for sweetness.

He pulled away and raised a small wooden jug. He drank, never taking his eyes off mine. Then he leaned in and gave me a drink from his own mouth. It was mead, and it warmed my insides all the way down.

Ragnar had stopped spanking me. He rested his hand on my burning bottom.

"How goes her punishment?" Loki asked. "Thirsty work?"

Ragnar grunted.

Loki raised the flask. "I have mead but no cup," he mused. "But I have found a better vessel. Shall I show you?"

Ragnar tipped me up to sit in his lap. His big hands slid down my front, cupping my breasts, settling me against his bare chest. His cock rested in the crevice of my heated buttocks.

With a wicked gleam in his green eye, Loki poured mead into my mouth. Whisking the skin away, he slanted his head to fit his lips over mine and licked the sweet honey drink from the insides of my mouth.

My tongue fought with his for a taste. When we broke apart, my chest was heaving but Loki was laughing.

"Try it," he told Ragnar.

Ragnar tilted my head back and Loki poured the mead carefully into my mouth. Before I could swallow, Ragnar turned my head with a fist in my hair and sealed his lips over mine. His tongue thrust in, penetrating my mouth. I arched up into the kiss, moaning a little. Needing more. When he pulled back, I felt empty. My cunny hummed with an answering ache.

"Sweet." Ragnar's voice was hoarse.

My head would have drooped if he hadn't held it aloft.

"More."

Loki filled my mouth and took a taste, licking neatly at

my lips. A little mead dribbled out, running down my chin. Ragnar turned my head this way and that, capturing each bead of honey-colored liquid with gentle kisses.

"Rosalind," he growled against my skin. His beard was wet.

My head lolled, and Loki steadied me.

"Drunk already, little troublemaker?"

I opened my mouth and he let a little mead spill in, but most of it ran down my chin and formed a river between my breasts.

Loki let out a breathless chuckle. He knelt before us and licked up my belly. I reached for his dark head and he caught my wrists. His tongue probed my belly button, followed by the lightest nipping of his teeth.

He dragged his mouth lower, following the tracks of mead further down between my legs.

There, he brushed the sensitive skin of my sex, finding the smooth surface wet. His fingers probed and spread my lower lips.

"I have found a cup. A Rosalind-shaped cup." He sounded delighted.

Ragnar didn't scoff at Loki's silliness. The big warrior was too busy molding his rough palm to my breast, stroking my sticky skin until my hips drew up with wanting.

"A pretty pink cup." Loki smacked my cunny lightly. "Shall I drink from it?" His thumb found a sweet, aching spot and rubbed it lightly. A tremor ran through my taut belly.

"Lay her down," Ragnar said.

Both he and Loki eased my limp body down onto the cloak. Loki remained between my legs, rubbing his nimble fingers over the shaven apex of my folds, caressing my cunny. Ragnar leaned my upper body on his lap so he could continue to play with my breasts. My body was stretched out between them, shining in the firelight. My skin was sticky with fluid and kisses.

Loki lay down and kissed my cunny. He held the jug of mead up and let the liquid pour slowly over my lower half. His dark head rested on my leg, his mouth close to my aching center. His tongue lapped up the rivers of mead, swiping up and down my skin.

My toes scrunched and my whole body drew up, on the edge of a shaking climax.

"No." Loki took his mouth away and slapped the wet place between my legs. A *thwack* echoed around the glade.

I gasped. "Oh, please."

"No coming without permission." Ragnar squeezed my breast, hard. I swiveled my hips, whimpering.

"Do that again." Loki set his mouth at my cunny again. "She responds beautifully to pain." His tongue swiped up my folds, and he licked his lips. "Cream and mead."

Ragnar grunted and reached down, swiping his fingers along my cunny, collecting the mixture of moisture there. He sucked his fingers. "Good." He reached down for more.

"Wait." Loki slapped my center again. "Now."

Ragnar rubbed between my legs, hard.

"Nice and pink." Loki lay on his belly, squinting at my sex.

"Delicious." Ragnar fed me his fingers. I tasted myself, along with the mead. "Turn her over," he said.

They propped me on my hands and knees. Somehow, I remained upright.

"Time for her to earn her reward." Ragnar had his cock free from his breeches. It was long and straight, jutting out of a thatch of blond hair as if it was searching for me. "Here, now." He cupped my cheek, supporting my head as he fed me his cock. "Easy now."

His cedar scent surrounded me as his cock filled my mouth. I licked tentatively at his heated flesh.

"There, that's the way." He pushed further into my mouth. My body tightened with surprise, and I choked. He withdrew so only his head rested between my lips. "Again. You can take me. I will teach you." His hands were strong but gentle on either side of my face. I lay with my head against his strong thigh, panting, and he let me rest.

When I was ready, I curled my tongue around the tip of his cock.

His blue eyes shone with gold sparks. "Good girl." A jolt went through me. I let him push his cock deeper into my mouth. I wanted, needed, to hear his praise again.

In his place behind me, Loki was busy. Liquid dripped over my back, flowing over my bottom. I couldn't turn my head but didn't have to. He was still anointing me with mead. The small jug seemed bottomless.

The liquid washed over my heated backside. Loki licked at my punished flesh, his tongue soothing and cooling.

He parted my rear cheeks and poured the mead directly on my private hole. His face nudged between my cheeks, his stubble scratching as he licked up the sensitive seam and pressed his tongue against my crinkled flesh. I jerked but Ragnar held my head fast. I could only tense on all fours as Loki's tongue stimulated me. Dark pleasure licked through my body.

"So sweet," Loki murmured. He took his face away and gripped each of my bottom cheeks, squeezing and smacking, letting them bounce together.

I moaned around Ragnar's cock in my mouth.

"Hold her still," Loki said to Ragnar, and Ragnar took a tighter grip on my hair.

A finger probed my bottom hole and I squealed, hunching forward. The movement pushed Ragnar's cock deeper, and he let out a harsh groan that echoed in the night.

"So tight and hot," Loki said with satisfaction. His finger was deep in my bottom, swirling around

I tried to protest and it came out a humming sound around Ragnar's cock.

"Thor's balls," Ragnar snarled to the sky.

"Not Thor's," Loki corrected.

Ragnar held my head still as he pushed his cock deeper, growling, "That's it. Take it all."

I did my best, drawing air through my nose as Ragnar's muscled abdomen came closer. His cock speared my throat. I held still for a moment, then my body seized, panicking for breath. Ragnar drew out, letting me cough and suck in air. His cock tapped my cheek and I turned my head to put my mouth on it again.

"Good girl," Ragnar crooned.

Now something was brushing my cunny—large and hard and hot. I dropped my hips, trying to get more stimulation. "No, no, keep your bottom up." Loki's cock went away and he slapped my rear with his free hand. His other was still probing my ass.

"Rosalind." Ragnar cradled my chin, turning my face up even with my mouth stretched around his cock. "Look at me, lass."

He stroked my hair out of my face, a curiously tender gesture from the warrior who'd been choking me with his rod only a moment ago.

"You don't run from me. You don't leave me. We belong together."

I blinked.

"Say it." He leaned forward, and his hand smacked my upturned bottom.

He pulled back so his cock popped out of my lax mouth. His hand gripped my chin, wrenching my head up to meet his bright gold eyes.

"You don't leave me," he growled, and I could hear the monster lying under his words. "You belong to me, Rosalind. You are mine. I will never let any harm come to you."

I opened my mouth but only a gasp came out.

Lower down, Loki dragged my hips down until my cunny was resting on his face. I ground against him.

His tongue hit the perfect spot, and my eyes rolled back as a blaze of pleasure flamed through me.

Ragnar waited until he could steady my head, then thrust into my mouth. Once, twice, again. Pumping, filling my mouth. His cum spurted down my throat, and I drank him down. His seed dripped down the corner of my chin and he scooped it onto his thumb and fed it to me.

"Well done." He stroked my cheek. "Do you need to rest?"

I shook my head. "More."

I had one night, and one night alone. I would let the Berserkers do with me what they would, and take everything they would give.

* * *

Ragnar

ROSALIND'S bare body shimmered in the firelight. As always, every time I looked at her, my breath caught as if I beheld some never before seen wonder.

She was a goddess in human form, her hair a honey-colored waterfall, her skin made of moonlight and mead.

I regretted what I'd told her. I could never take a mate. But Rosalind was mine, as much as I was hers.

As for Loki, well, I'd kill him if I could. But tonight he'd proved useful, erecting a barrier between us and the rest of the world.

As if he'd heard my thoughts, he raised his head and winked at me. I glared at him.

"My turn for her mouth." Loki tugged her around. "There you are, sweetness," he crooned, cupping her face and guiding her onto his cock.

Tomorrow belonged to fate, the quest, and the fight for our lives. But tonight belonged to us.

Rosalind's bright head bobbed in front of Loki as she crouched between us. That left her bottom upturned right in front of me. Her curved rear and haunches were streaked with red—evidence of her punishment at my hand. I rubbed the skin, admiring my work. Reaching over her bottom, I settled my palm on her back and pushed it down. This propped her rear even higher. The seam of her bottom split like a ripe peach, dripping nectar. My mouth watered, and my fangs grew razor sharp.

Rosalind broke off Loki's cock and looked back at me, curious.

"Don't mind him," Loki tapped his wet staff against her cheek until she took him in her mouth again.

I bowed to lick her dripping sex, swiping my tongue between her folds, all the way up to her tiny, winking bum hole. She tasted of earth and sweetness. I growled against her cunny and her body shuddered.

My cock strained towards her. I could wait no longer.

Gripping her hips, I set my cock against her entrance and plowed forward in one stroke. The force drove her further onto Loki's cock. He groaned, his lean body growing taut as a bowstring. His mouth opened in a snarl, and showed a flash of bone-white fang. Our beasts rising to the fore, ready to mark our mate. Perhaps he was a Berserker after all.

My cock throbbed deep in Rosalind's sweet cunny. Her body squeezed me until pleasure blackened my vision. That is what this woman did to me. One stroke, and my cock threatened to burst like a boy's.

Across Rosalind's sleek body, Loki raised his chin in challenge. I gritted my teeth and slid almost all the way out of Rosalind's perfect sex. Loki pushed his hips forward, and Rosalind rocked back. Her cunny sheathed my sword once more. My growl echoed around the glade.

Loki's narrow face was half in shadow, but moonlight glinted off his cheek when he grinned. "Again."

We both rocked in opposing rhythm, moving Rosalind's body between us. She was a lean, golden vessel for our pleasure. As we sped up our thrusts, her body trembled. She tipped into ecstasy and became pure pleasure. Her cunny squeezed my cock as if it would draw me deeper inside her. If I had my way, we would be joined forever, like this.

My abdomen tightened and I curled over her, pulling her against me until our skin sealed together with sweat. Tension tightened in the small of my back. Across the way, Loki grunted his pleasure to the stars. I thrust one final time and let my climax burst forth. Pleasure bloomed in a knot at the base of my spine, radiating outwards in runners of searing delight.

Between us, Rosalind sagged. Loki caught her shoulders and supported her, murmuring soothing nonsense. I grit my teeth and pulled out of her body's hot embrace. She toppled over.

Loki and I stretched her out between us and bathed her with cool water.

She barely stirred.

"I'll take first watch," Loki said. He squeezed Rosalind's slim ankle before he rose and left me to gather her in my arms. Her honeyed scent surrounded me as I wrapped myself around her.

I busied myself brushing her gold hair back from her face.

Her cheek curved and her eyes fluttered open. "When I first met you, I thought you were a brute." Her hand came to my cheek and found my smiling lips tucked behind my beard.

"I am." I hitched her closer. "Remember, I'm a monster."

"My monster," she murmured, and curled into me. Her cheek lay on my chest. Her body relaxed. She found peace in my arms, totally trusting.

I closed my eyes, savoring this perfect moment. "When I first met you, the scent of the Corpse king was upon you."

I felt her flinch and laid my hand on her head to soothe her. "It's all right, Rosalind. Do you know who you smell like now?"

"No." Her voice was very small.

I ducked my head to find her ear. "Me. You bear my scent, and I intend to keep it that way."

She sighed, and the tension went out of her shoulders. "What about Loki?"

I sniffed. "You smell like him, too. I try not to think about that."

Her laugh huffed against my chest. Her body relaxed even further, and she fell asleep between one breath and the next.

CHAPTER 8

I DID NOT WANT to sleep. I wanted to remain awake and treasure this moment. But both Rosalind and I needed rest. In the morning, I would rise and continue on the quest beside her. Tonight, I could only hold her and pray it would not be the last time.

My hopes that Rosalind would sleep without dreams were dashed when she awoke with her mouth open in a silent scream. I raced to draw her into my arms, calling her name as her body thrashed against me.

"Rosalind." I held her tight, steadying her. "It's all right. You're safe."

She came awake with a gasp. For a second, her eyes flashed moonstone bright. Then the light faded, leaving her frightened face.

"I dreamt the Corpse King won. We all died." She curled into me, pressing her forehead to my chest.

"It was only a dream. It will not happen." I cast about and finally snapped at Loki, "Tell her!"

"He's right." Loki crouched beside us. His hand cuffed her ankle. "There's still hope, Rosalind."

Finally, she sat up, wiping her face. "I need to wash." She stumbled blindly towards her dress. Last night, Loki had brushed it off and hung it on a bush.

I turned away to give her privacy. When she returned from the river, I handed her a clean, flat stone I'd found to use as a plate for the fish I'd baked.

"I'm not hungry." She tried to refuse the meal, but Loki and I insisted.

A few half-hearted bites, and she stared into the fire. Her face was wan and pale, her eyes haunted, as if she was still in the grip of the dream.

I touched her wrist. "I will not let you die."

She and Loki shared a glance. I fought the urge to insert myself between them. "It's no use." Rosalind set down her plate. "You cannot keep me alive."

"I can. I will," I vowed.

Rosalind rose, shaking out her dress. "It's no use," she said in a brisk, practical tone. "The quest ends in my death. The witches foretold it."

"It's true," Loki said.

"No," I snarled at him. We both came to our feet at the same time, and if the moment were not so fraught, if Rosalind was not so distraught, I would have launched myself at him to beat him into the ground. I did not like what he was saying. Why was he taking her side? "How could you say that? Are you giving up?"

"It's fate," Rosalind whispered.

"We make our own fate."

"Like you make yours?" Loki shot back.

I bared my teeth at him. "That is different." I glared at

Loki, willing him not to say any more.

Rosalind set her hands on either side of my face and tugged my gaze away from Loki's.

"Go home, Ragnar. Find a mate, and live happily. That is why I am on this quest. Not for myself, but for my sister, and the rest of the spaewives. So they may have a good life and be free of the Corpse King's threat." She looked even smaller and more fragile this morning. Last night, she'd been a goddess, this morning, she was a young, frightened woman.

"I will not leave you," I told her.

"Go home, Ragnar," Loki called from across the clearing. He'd spent the morning erasing all but a few strategically placed runes from the dirt. Now he stood with his foot propped on a stone, sharpening his many knives. "The Alphas sent you to pursue Rosalind and drag her back. If you will not do that then you have no more part here." He lowered his voice. "You know she cannot be your mate."

"I know that," I snapped. I searched for a pack bond so I might tell Loki silently: *shut up.*

But he did not get my unspoken message. "It was a good deal the Alphas offered," he continued. "You find the runaway, and she becomes your mate."

"What?" Rosalind's gasp rang out, the betrayal written on her face.

* * *

ROSALIND

RAGNAR GLARED, his body quivering as if it took all his effort not to leap across the glade and cut Loki down.

"Did he not tell you, Rosalind?" Loki went on as if oblivious to the warrior staring murder at his face. "The quest was to find you, and whoever won would be rewarded. You were the reward."

"It doesn't matter," Ragnar growled.

"How can you say that?" I burst out. It did not surprise me that I would have been given as a trophy to a winner. That was to be expected. What mattered was that Ragnar didn't tell me. "It matters to me—"

"I would not have accepted it," Ragnar said.

"It?" I put my hands on my hips.

"You." He scrubbed a hand over his face. "The reward. I would not have accepted you as a mate."

This was worse than betrayal. Ragnar couldn't have hurt me more if he'd stabbed me. I stiffened my features, making my face cold. "You don't want me as a mate."

"That's not what he said," Loki murmured. "Look at him."

Ragnar was half turned away from us, his hands curled into fists. His muscles quivered in silent strain. His shoulders were hunched halfway to his ears.

"He wants you, Rosalind," Loki explained. "That's the problem. He wants you too much."

"Do not speak for me," Ragnar growled, and I flinched. His voice was thick with the guttural tones of the beast.

Loki raised his hands palms up. "No threat offered, brother."

Ragnar's roar shook the glade. "Be silent!"

"Ragnar," I whispered. "Please."

Another roar, and he stalked off to the edge of the glade, stopping just short of the wall of mist.

After a glance at Loki, I followed.

"Don't come near," he snarled without turning. Black fur grew along his arms.

I paid no heed to his warning. I waited at his back, close enough to touch him. Eventually, the fur disappeared. When Ragnar spoke again, his voice was normal.

"I had a warrior brother once. A better man than I. And the beast..." He fell silent.

I took his arm, stroking the skin where fur had sprouted only a moment before. "I'm sorry." He'd lost his warrior brother. For a Berserker, that was like losing part of his soul.

And I'd once tried to goad him by asking why he didn't have a warrior brother. I was a callous fool.

"I could not save him. No one could." Ragnar stared out at the trees, gazing at a distant memory. "I could not pull him back from the brink. In the end, the only way to stop him was to cleave his head from his body. So I did."

Merely touching his arm was no longer enough. We'd lain together; he needed me now. I stepped in front of him and slid my arms around his waist. After a moment, he clutched me to him. I let myself lean on him, cheek to his chest. "How did you survive?" The bonds formed between warriors to keep them from madness. If one succumbed... the other was soon to follow.

Ragnar's hand came to cradle my head. "I did not think it would be long before the beast consumed me. I knew the Alphas would be quick to put me down. I welcomed it. I was in darkness..." He tugged on my hair, pulling my head back to lift my face to his. "And then I saw you."

I shook my head.

"I couldn't save myself. But I could try to save you."

"Last night, you said I belonged to you."

"I should not have said that."

"So you don't want me."

"You know I do." He pressed his forehead to mine. His growl rumbled in his chest, under my palms. "You are the only thing in the world I want. And I cannot have you."

"Ragnar," I said in a shaking voice, "you should choose another—"

"No. There is no one for me but you."

"But…" I was crying now, "I cannot…" I could not be with him. "I have to…"

"I know. You have your quest. I have mine." He thumbed away my tears. "I am a weapon. I will go where I will cause the most damage before I meet my death."

I would have wrenched myself away from him, but he would not let me go. "No." I struggled, my hands grappling with him even though I only wanted to hold him tight.

"Shhh." He pulled me close again. "You don't know what it's like, at the end. The madness takes over. You become the beast. There's no return. When it is time, Loki will finish me."

I turned my head to glare at Loki, who now hovered at our elbows. "You knew about this," I accused him.

Loki shrugged. "I knew what the witches foretold about you, as well. You are both so determined to walk to your deaths. It seems I am the only one who wants to survive."

Ragnar growled, and turned us so we had some privacy.

I tugged on Ragnar's neck, drawing his head close to mine. "I could do this if I knew you would go on. I want you to survive, live a good life. That's why I'm doing this—for my sister. The spaewives. And…" my whisper hitched on a sob, "you."

"I know, lass. It's not to be. But this quest, the enemy… we face them together." He nuzzled my cheek, his lips finding my ear. "Promise me." The scrape of his blond beard and his whisper sent a shiver down my spine.

I gripped him harder. "I promise."

"I know when you lie," Ragnar growled. He gripped my chin, forcing my gaze to his. The gold light in his eyes seared me.

I bit my lip because I could not promise not to leave him behind. The first chance I had, I would run, and hope that he survived.

"Come," Loki said. "There is not much time. We must be off." As usual, he was clad all in black. He'd left his cloak and packs behind. For weapons, he held a staff carved with runes, and wore a wide black leather belt strapped across his chest, holding a dozen daggers of ranging sizes.

"I'm ready," Ragnar grunted. He stepped away from me and took up his axes, gripping one in each hand. His nails had thickened to claws. His eyes glittered bright with the gold of the beast. He would turn soon, and become a monster. According to what he'd told me, he would not turn back. This was the end for him. "Rosalind." He motioned, and I fell into step between them.

My hands were free. I had no weapon, nothing but the moonstone dagger still on a leather thong around my neck. I could only hope the Corpse King's servants wouldn't be drawn to the moonstone

Underneath the weight of the moonstone, my heart beat very, very fast.

We marched onward, Ragnar at my back, and Loki scouting ahead. With each step, my own thoughts mocked me. Who was I to think I could complete this quest?

"This way." Loki beckoned and I hastened my steps, struggling to climb a rocky hill.

It was too late to turn back, but this wasn't going to work. I couldn't go on knowing that I would lose Ragnar. As for Loki… he had said that if he died in this life, he died forever. I did not quite know what that meant but I did not want him to die.

"Wait," I said, but a rumble ripped from Ragnar's chest and drowned me out.

As we rounded a crop of boulders, the stench of the draugr hit me. The smell blended with the spiced scent of the Corpse King's magic. Stretching before us in a grey, stinking sea were tens of thousands of undead soldiers. Just like in my dream.

"So many of them." The words turned to dust in my parched mouth. Every few feet, blue flames flickered over the soldiers' heads. The mage's magic keeping them in line.

"Beyond them—do you see? In the mist?" Loki pointed. Beyond the ranks of draugr, a heavy grey cloud covered the earth. A thick wall of mist, much like the one Loki had woven around us last night. Only this spell was a hundred times as big. "He has hidden his fortress. That is our destination."

"Let's go." Ragnar hoisted his axe.

"You fool," Loki made the insult sound almost fond. "You think you can fight them all?"

"I can try." Ragnar's eyes glinted bright as a jarl's torch.

"If you go straight through them, how long will Rosalind survive?" Loki pointed out.

"I must walk in of my own strength," I repeated what the witches told me.

"There's a way around," Loki murmured. He pointed to the south, where a silver line glinted in the early sun. "Along the river. The draugr do not like to cross it."

"How long will it take?" I rasped. My mouth was filled with ashes.

"We will arrive by nightfall."

"Let us be off then," I said before Ragnar could protest.

Head down, I marched behind Loki. My back bowed, and it became harder to breathe as we ventured deeper into the Corpse King's power. We crept along, hiding as best we could. The Corpse King's servants had cut down all trees, and stripped the land. They must have burned much of it, for the air had a smokey tang. Now and again we came upon scorched patches of earth. Nothing grew. No birds sang. The Corpse King had turned this place into a barren hell-hole.

Even the river, when we reached it, was fouled and sludge-like. We dared not drink its water.

"This is the fate of the world," Loki murmured, almost to himself. "If we do not stop the Corpse—"

"Hush," I snapped. "Do not speak his name. Even now, the stones might be listening."

"You think a little silence will change our fate?"

"I will do my best," I said, glancing up at the column of thick mist that loomed ever closer. "It's all I can do. You can run, Loki, if you like."

"I think I'll stay."

"Even knowing you might die?" I picked up my skirts a little higher off the charred earth.

Loki fell into step beside me. He was playing with a small dagger, tossing it into the air and catching it without cutting himself. "I've never died before. It might be interesting."

"This is a game to you?"

"No." He caught the dagger and used the tip to scratch his eyebrow. "This is the one time where the stakes are too high. I will do my best to help you, Rosalind. I give you my word."

"Promises can be broken," I murmured.

Loki grinned and went back to tossing the dagger.

I watched him a moment, then snatched the weapon from the air before he could catch it. Using the tricks he'd taught me, I flipped it over and around both my hands, and slipped it into my sleeve. I raised my hands palm up to show the dagger was gone.

"Well done. Not enough to fool me, of course." Loki winked, and the dagger was in his hand, no longer in my sleeve. "But good enough to fool most."

"Would that you had more time to teach me."

"That's the trouble with being mortal. There's not enough time. Every moment matters." He rubbed his head. "Every action can lead to life or death. I am not used to things mattering."

"And as a god, nothing matters to you?"

"No," he sighed. "I suppose that's why I am here. To see if I have a heart after all."

"If you do, I hope you find it," I murmured. I was glad I'd met Loki, even if it was only for a short time.

"If anyone could stir my heart, Rosalind, it would be you," he purred, letting his gaze glide over me, head to foot. I was filthy from the soot, my hair clumped with sweat and dirt. But I still flushed like a lady-in-waiting under his scrutiny. "But as it were, you only stirred my—"

"The enemy," Ragnar's grunt cut into our conversation. "Draugr. Ahead."

We were between the river and a man-made hillock of earth. Ragnar crept up the mound and crawled the last few feet on his belly. Loki and I did the same.

Just over the hill, the draugr stood in silent rows, waiting for the order to attack.

They were so close, I could make out the sooty smudges on their weapons.

"Is there a way around them?" I asked in the barest whisper.

"Not this time," Loki said calmly. "The river curves and leads away. We cannot get any closer."

"If we can't go around them, then we go through them." Ragnar slid his axe to point higher up the hill. "Rosalind, be ready to run."

My heartbeat pounded as I pressed myself against the bare earth. Ahead, the Corpse King's magic was thick as perfume. The last time it had been so strong, the Corpse King had projected himself right in front of me. I closed my eyes and felt his bony fingers on my face.

"Rosalind?" Loki's murmur drew me back.

"Yes." My voice was faint. "I'm ready."

Something made me glance behind me. Behind us, creeping along the river, were more draugr.

I must have made a noise of warning, because Ragnar and Loki both turned.

"We're trapped," Loki said sharply. "We must go."

Loki and Ragnar rose to their feet as one. Ragnar hefted his axe, ready to swing it in a deadly cyclone.

But Loki stepped forward, quicker than the eye could see. He threw a dagger. It sailed slowly, end over end, into the waiting host. Between the moment the blade left Loki's fingers, and the moment it touched down onto the earth between the ranks of draugr, the sky darkened.

Lightning crackled down, splitting the air in a blinding river of white light. The lightning struck the dagger, and splintered. Jagged lines of pure power struck the ranks of undead soldiers. Thunder rolled. Several draugr fell.

Ragnar and I looked at Loki, our mouths hanging open.

"I have a few tricks up my sleeve." Loki's smile was as sharp as a blade. "Rosalind, follow our lead."

I gathered my skirts. They felt heavy in my hands.

Loki strode down the hillock, a dagger in each hand. Distant flashes of lightning silhouetted his dark form.

Ragnar roared. Swinging his axe, he raced down the hill, passing Loki. He rushed into the ranks of the undead and kept going. Bodies flew. I followed, racing into the path Ragnar and Loki cleaved before me.

Looking back, it seems impossible that we made our way through the ranks of the draugr. I can only wonder if the Corpse King knew we were coming, and welcomed it, and so forbade his soldiers to fight.

In the moment, in the thick of things, I had no time to think. Loki had said that the draugr wanted me to go to the Corpse King, that the mage wanted the moonstone. It must have been true but in the heat of the moment, with the press of the draugr's stench upon us, the fight seemed endless and unwinnable.

As I followed the warriors through the draugr, my horror grew and my steps faltered. Loki had to return to my side long enough to catch my arm and pull me along. With his free hand, he slashed at any draugr unlucky enough to come close. Ragnar's axe rose and fell like a scythe, cutting through the lines of soldiers. Rank upon rank, they came alive as one and moved with a dry, creaking sound. The lightning struck again and again, igniting the undead.

Loki had to let go of me to fend off a squadron. I stumbled. Bony fingers caught my arms. I thrashed, to no avail. The soldiers dragged me a few feet.

"Ragnar," I cried. I caught my breath when he turned. He was no longer a man. His eyes glowed in the face of a black-furred beast towering ten feet high. His axe looked like a toy in his hand. He flung the weapon into the ranks of the enemy, taking out ten draugr at a time. He loped past me, beastly paws extended. His claws ripped through the closest soldiers.

"Got you," Loki was at my back, lifting me easily. He spun around, and carried me like a bride across the battlefield. Bones and debris crunched underfoot.

I wanted to close my eyes, but it seemed wrong not to bear witness to the carnage these two warriors wrought.

The battle was not over. There were more draugr closing in, blocking our way back. Not that I needed a way back. Ahead of us loomed the wall of mist—a long, smoke-like column hiding the Corpse King's fortress. That was where my quest would end.

But for Loki and Ragnar, it did not have to end here.

"Let me down." I struggled in Loki's arms. "I must walk in of my own volition."

"We don't know what's behind the mist. You could be walking for miles." But he set me down, and darted forward to fight the draugr who stood in my path.

I picked up my skirts and followed, keeping as close to Loki as I dared. My head down, I didn't notice we were on a hill until he threw the last of the draugr down it.

"We're clear. Look."

Ahead was nothing but barren land, sloping down into the wall of mist.

"Let me go alone," I said.

"No," a growl sounded from the foot of the hill.

Somehow the monster that was Ragnar had fought his way clear of the soldiers. He climbed to our sides, half walking, half crawling on the beast's burly, fur-covered arms.

"We go together," Loki said. I nodded. With the beast on my right and Loki on my left, I raced down the hill towards the mist.

"Hold fast to me." Loki grabbed my arm as we hurtled forward towards the billowing grey.

I could not shake him off. Together, we plowed into the fog.

The magic mist enveloped me like mud. I couldn't see. I couldn't breathe. It was like being buried alive.

"What is happening?" I tried to scream. My hands clawed at the fog in front of me, but the grey did not clear. I was trapped. "No!" Panic beat in my breast. I thrashed but it was like moving in water. The magic surrounded me, closing in. There was no way out.

Someone tugged me forward. I fought, at first.

"Rosalind!" I thought I heard a muffled whisper in the mist.

It was Loki. He was still holding my arm.

If it weren't for Loki hauling me forward, I might never

have broken free. Somehow, he pulled me out of the viscous grey and into the bright day.

The mist cleared, and we both lay, hacking, on the grass. I dashed my hands over my face, wiping my eyes as if I could wipe away the mist. Only after I'd taken a few breaths of clean air did I calm.

"Thank you," I said.

Loki nodded. His own chest heaved. His green eye was wild. The spell had affected him too. We both sat on the green grass, in a pleasant forest glade. Trees rustled in the wind. Birds chirped in their branches. It was like another world.

The beautiful day did not reassure me.

"Ragnar?" I turned. "Where is Ragnar?"

There was no sign of the monster. Was he still stuck in the mist?

A huge, golden-eyed wolf padded out of the forest. I'd never seen such a giant beast. Wolves were bigger than dogs, but this wolf was bigger than an ordinary one by far.

"Ragnar?"

At my call, he slunk closer. The sunlight dappled his grey and brown fur.

"Ragnar." I held out a hand, inviting him forward. I'd never seen him in wolf form. But I knew it was him.

"Wait." Loki tugged me back. "The madness is upon him."

"He would never hurt me." I opened my arms, and the wolf closed the gap. I hugged his neck, pushing my face into the thick ruff. He smelled like cedar.

"I'm glad you survived," I whispered.

The wolf drew back and licked at my face. The rasp of his rough tongue reassured me.

After a moment, I tugged myself up, with the wolf's help.

The air in the glade was warm, lush, and green, and gilded with gentle sunlight.

"What is this place?" I asked. It looked too beautiful to be the Corpse King's domain.

"The inner sanctum. My guess is the fortress lies that way." Loki pointed into the forest. For a moment the birds stopped chirping, then they resumed.

I shivered. Beautiful or no, something wasn't right about this place.

"I suppose we should keep going." I couldn't keep the reluctance out of my voice. "Perhaps it will be easy from now on."

"Wait." Loki stopped me with a hand on my arm. "Do you hear that?"

The birds had gone silent again.

Deep in the forest a creaking sound echoed.

"Something's coming," I said.

The wolf straightened, teeth bared. His fur rose on end and he growled, long and low.

Beyond the first line of trees, something was moving. The trees beyond shuddered, their leaves rustling.

Loki and Ragnar stepped in front of me.

Out of the forest flew a long grey bone. It bounced on the lawn and came to a stop a few feet away. Another bone followed, landing on the first with a clatter. We all stared.

Another bone and another, until the pile grew. Blue light limned the gruesome mound.

"Can we go around it?" I ventured forward, but Loki raised a hand. Something shifted in the pile. The light of the Corpse King's magic flared upwards, and the bones flew into a formation. More bones flew out of the forest to join the rest, and the magic built them into a towering shape. It had a broad back like a horse, and legs and a long, long neck. And when it opened its bare, bony jaw, it spat blue fire.

"Thor's balls," Loki grunted, and unsheathed two knives.

"A bone dragon." He cast a glance to Ragnar. "Can you transform?"

The wolf shook his head.

"Wonderful," Loki muttered. "It's up to me to fight the final guardian. Rosalind, you'd best stay out of the way."

The dragon lurched forward slowly on half-formed legs. If I hadn't seen it, I wouldn't have believed the creature could exist. It was no more than a bundle of bones, bound together with blue light.

I stepped to the side, closer to the wall of mist. I took care not to let the grey fog touch me.

My fingers slid into my pocket. The rune balls lay there.

"Loki," I called. "Can you do any magic?"

He rolled his shoulders and tilted his head until his neck cracked. "I can try."

I clutched a rune ball in my hand. If I could help, I would.

The wolf darted forward for the first attack. Ragnar dashed between the dragon's legs, snapping. He tore into the creature, tossing bones aside. Blue light illuminated his fur. The dragon somehow turned and kicked out, and wolf Ragnar went flying. He landed on the grass and rolled to his feet. Unharmed.

But the bones he'd torn from the dragon's body twitched. For a moment, they quivered like iron nails near a lodestone. Then the blue light flashed, and the bones Ragnar had torn from the dragon flew back and were re-absorbed into the bone formation.

"Damn," Loki said. "We must find a way to take it apart and stop it from animating again." He snapped his fingers. "Salt."

Ragnar the wolf was already attacking the dragon, tearing at its legs again.

Loki ran behind, dodging the dragon's newly formed tail.

A few bones landed on the grass, tossed there by Ragnar.

Loki threw a handful of salt over them. The bones twitched, and then went still.

"Aha!" He turned to grin at me, triumphant.

The dragon's long neck snapped around. It opened its bony maw.

"Loki, look out," I screamed.

A furred shape slammed into Loki before the blue fire caught him. Wolf Ragnar and Loki rolled together over the grass, rising to their feet in time to dance out of the way of the bone dragon's flailing tail.

Loki called across the clearing to the furred warrior. "You saved my life, wolf. I won't forget it."

Together, they attacked the bone dragon. Ragnar's fangs ripped bones away, out of the magic formation. Loki salted them. Piles of bones lay inert in the grass. The magic could not touch them.

Rosalind, someone whispered to me. A voice I'd heard many times before, in the dead of winter when I could not sleep. I gripped the front of my gown, checking to see if the dagger was still there.

Beyond the glade, the forest beckoned.

It was time to finish my quest. While the warriors were busy with the dragon, I could slip away. They would not die. They could fight their way back, through the mist, and together they would carve a path through the draugr so they could escape.

Come to me, the Corpse King whispered. I took a step forward, and another. The mist flared out as I passed it, as if trying to grab me. Herding me forward. I edged around the field of battle, dodging flying bones. The only sounds were the warriors' grunts and the clanking bones.

Eventually, I made my way close to the forest. Ragnar and Loki did not even notice.

Be safe, I willed them, and with one last glance, I turned to run.

"Rosalind," Loki shouted. He was on top of the dragon, riding its bony spine. The dragon lurched. Ragnar dodged the flailing tail and raked his claws into it, scattering more bones upon the grass.

"You must wait for us," Loki grunted, fighting to keep his balance.

"Go back," I shouted, motioning to the mist. "Save yourself."

"No," Loki snarled. "We must not be separated. If there is to be any hope, we must stay together. The witches foretold it!"

"There is no hope for me," I said. "You know that."

With a war cry, Loki steadied himself and poured salt right on the dragon's neck. Blue light flared, blinding me.

The dragon disintegrated, half the bones falling to the ground. The other half flew to form a cage around Ragnar and Loki.

"No!" Loki fought the bones, but his salt pouch lay on the trampled grass, empty. He and Ragnar tore the cage apart, only to have it reform around them.

Eventually, they would fight their way free and come after me.

I thrust my fingers into my pouch, where the witches had given me a few weapons. I would not use them on my enemy, but on my friends.

"No!" Loki shouted.

I pitched the smoke bombs to the ground. They exploded with a great crack that threw me backwards. Behind me, smoke billowed. Bits of bone rained down. A roar of rage drove me to my feet.

In the confusion, I whirled, and ran.

* * *

Loki

"Dammit, what is she thinking?" I muttered. The smoke from the rune stones cleared. The weapons helped blow one corner of the cage apart. Ragnar and I fought the rest of the bones. The wolf bit them, and I stomped them to powder. Slowly, we worked to free ourselves.

"I was supposed to help her," I complained as I worked. "Little ninny, running full bore ahead with no regard for her life."

Ragnar the wolf barked.

"Don't shout at me." I glared at him. He tossed a bone to me, and I snapped it in half. "We had a plan, and she ruined it. True, the witches told her she would not survive this quest. But there are many things that can turn fate. I'm not sure what, but something might come to me."

We were almost clear of the cage. I kicked at the bony lattice, and it fell apart. Blue magic curled half-heartedly around the pieces.

I stomped on them, just in case. "We make our own fate, someone once told me." I winked at Ragnar. The wolf did not look amused. Indeed, there was an accusing light in his golden eyes.

"Well, what would you have me do?" I waved a bone. "She left me behind. Just because she's determined to be a hero doesn't mean I have to follow suit."

The wall of mist. I could leave now, and return to the witches. No one would fault me.

"I have to stay alive," I mused to myself. "It would be so sad if I died."

A cyclone of magic picked up, drawing the bones into a

tower. Ragnar and I both rushed it, making short work of the remaining bones.

Something prickled in my side. I touched my fingers to my jerkin, and they came away washed in brilliant red. I cursed.

Ragnar barked.

"Just some blood," I answered. "Common among humans, I'm told. Hope the wound isn't fatal."

The wolf cocked his head. I didn't like the way he was staring at my blood. I wiped my fingers on my breeches, and swiped up a fallen dagger.

"You should return, Ragnar." I nodded to the wall of mist. "You've done all you can."

The wolf bared his teeth at me. Then he turned and trotted in the direction Rosalind had run.

Have you ever done something for anyone other than yourself?

"Thor's tiny balls," I grunted, and followed.

It seemed I would have to be a hero after all.

* * *

ROSALIND

I CRASHED THROUGH THE FOREST, stumbling a little as I ran. The forest was quiet, lush and green, and achingly lovely. I didn't dare stop. *Would Ragnar and Loki ever forgive me?*

The day was warm and fine, the forest filled with welcoming birdsong. I raced through a glade, crushing bluebells under my boots. I'd run like this all the way to the gates of the Corpse King's fortress if I had to.

It didn't matter what happened to me. I had saved them.

My heart fluttered, a panicked bird in the cage of my

chest. I forced my steps to slow. My desperation didn't match the happy, sunny day.

Ragnar and Loki would be fine.

The more I walked, the calmer I felt. The grass seemed greener, the bluebells bluer. Overhead, the trees parted to show a clear sky. What had I found strange about this place? It tugged at my memory but I turned my thoughts away from it.

All would be well. I simply had to find the Corpse King, and my quest would be done. I could rest.

Why had I been so worried about the quest? My thoughts slipped from me like silver fishes in a stream, swimming away.

After a while, I came up to a brook, clear water rippling over the flat river stones. If I wanted, I could kneel and drink the fresh liquid but I curiously felt no hunger or thirst.

I'd been covered with dust and bits of ash, but now my dress looked clean. My hands and arms should have been smudged with soot, but the smooth, pale skin looked freshly scrubbed. My nails were unbroken. I leaned over the brook for a moment. My reflection showed my narrow face. I looked rested, regal. There was a brightness to my eyes. They almost glowed like moonstones.

I stared at my reflection, fiddling with the dagger under my bodice. There was something important about the dagger, but I could not remember what.

It didn't matter. The day rolled on, too pretty to waste. I did not know how long I walked. I followed the brook, soothed by its peaceful bubbling. Together, we meandered between lush crops of ferns and more bluebells.

Why had I thought that the Corpse King turned the world into a barren wasteland? This was the most beautiful forest I'd ever been in. It was perfect, almost like a garden. Perhaps the mage used his magic to create it.

A mage who created such a beautiful garden wouldn't be so terrible to meet. Would he?

My boots sank into the thick carpet of moss and flowers. Through the trees, I caught silver flashes of a waterfall. The brook was winding its way to it. I stepped around a cluster of birch, prickles running up my skin.

The waterfall crashed into a deep pool. The watery mist rose, cooling the air.

Beside the deep pool, staring at his reflection, lounged a young man. He was long in limb, with strong features and dark auburn hair.

I tucked myself against a birch tree, hugging the trunk for a moment as I peeked at the man. His face was flushed and healthy with the bloom of youth. He wore a long dark robe, like a priest or a scholar. This could be the mage's assistant.

As I left my hiding place and approached, the young man looked up and faced me with the full force of his beauty.

A wind stirred, brushing past me. I almost expected the wind to carry the stench of the draugr, but the air was clear.

The man had a spicy sort of scent. Not unpleasant.

"I am looking for the Corpse King," I said.

"Ah, yes." The young man rose, pale cheeks tinting a little red, as if embarrassed I'd caught him lounging. "He is here. You have found him. He dwells near here, in his castle."

"Is he your master?"

The man bowed his head. His hair was thick and full, shining like polished wood. Hints of red flashed in it as he moved. "Come, my lady, and I will bring you to him."

Our walk through the rest of the forest was slow and measured. We were heading uphill. Ahead loomed a mountain of mist. Every once in a while, the young man looked down and smiled at me.

Walk into the Corpse King's lair of your own volition. The memory came to me, but I had no idea what it meant.

The trees parted and with them, the mists cloaking the towering castle. Shining turrets stretched to the sky. The fortress was made of polished obsidian. It gleamed in the sunlight.

It reminded me of a dream I'd once had. And yet…

"It's smaller than I thought it would be," I said.

"It's not finished yet." The young man sounded a little annoyed.

I wanted to soothe him. "Will you show me inside?"

"It would be my pleasure. He held out a hand. I hesitated a moment, studying the unmarked palm. No callouses. His skin was young and supple, and when I placed my hand in his, it felt cool to the touch. Almost like stone.

But his beauty dazzled me, and I thought no more about his strange hands as I walked with him through the open gates.

 osalind

INSIDE THE CASTLE, braziers lit the way. There must have been some herb or mineral thrown onto the fire, because the flames burned blue, and a pungent smoke hung in the air. The eerie light reflected off the polished stone. Everything was obsidian—the floor, the walls, the ceiling, the huge columns that lined the great hall.

"It looks carved from stone."

"It was." The young man's voice echoed.

I kept my voice hushed, as if we were in church. "It is beautiful. How did this place come to be?"

"The mage is powerful. His magic has only grown."

Gemstones glittered in the columns we passed. I wanted to stop but the young man's steps didn't pause, so I kept pace with him. We were still holding hands.

"He seeks to free the world. Rule it. Create peace."

"At what cost peace?" I asked.

The young man quickened his steps. We turned a corner and entered a smaller hall. The light from the braziers created a tunnel of glowing blue. As we walked, my skirts disturbed the blue smoke that had settled in the corners. It curled before us, like a pet dogging our steps. No matter which way I turned, I couldn't see my shadow. It was as if it was swallowed up in the strange glow.

The scent of incense hung thick upon the air. *The scent of the Corpse King's magic.* Alarm buzzed in me but it fizzled out, leaving the heady calm.

The young man stopped and stood, watching me. His perfect face held only patience.

I knew then this wasn't an ordinary man, or an assistant.

I didn't want to look him in the eye, but something about his face drew me to him. "You wanted me to come here."

"I did." A smile played on his perfect lips. "I invited you to come sooner."

"I know."

"I thought you did not want to come."

"I was a captive of the Berserkers and did not know how to escape."

He tilted his head.

After a moment, he nodded.

"This way," he said, and led me through a door into a round tower and up a spiraling staircase.

"This is a beautiful castle. It took much power to build it," I said. Was I flattering him on purpose or simply telling the truth? There was a soft woolen layer of magic blanketing my mind.

"Yes," he said, and spared me a dazzling smile.

I ducked my head, my cheeks curving. It felt strange to smile. It was not like me. But for some reason, I wanted this young man to keep smiling at me.

It was an alien feeling. Deep down, under the layers of magic sedating me, the real Rosalind was screaming.

On Berserker Mountain, I never let anyone get close. I remained aloof. I used my words like blades and kept anyone from getting close to me. Only my sister clung to me, and that was because she knew I would do anything to protect her—even drive everyone else away.

The only ones who ever got close enough to peel back my layers of armor were Ragnar and Loki.

And now this mage, but something was not right about it. Or was it was I meant to come here all along?

"I thought if you would not come, I would invite another," the young man said.

I'd dreamt that too. If I refused the Corpse King, he would target another. My sister. I could not allow that. I had to save her.

And I had to force the Corpse King from my mind, and use the dagger.

One way or another, it all would end.

We climbed the stairs and at last entered a room with open windows. I knew if we looked out, we'd see some of the sights from my dream.

I stopped in the middle of the obsidian floor, unwilling to approach the unbarred windows.

"It will not be long until you rule," I said.

"No, Rosalind." His voice echoed, even here.

I put my back to the windows. "Let us speak plainly," I said. "You are the mage."

The young man bowed his head.

"You are younger than I expected."

"Magic preserves." He rubbed two long fingers together. Blue light sparked between them.

"But you need more."

"I always want more." Had his eyes always been blue? Or did they simply reflect the magic fire? "I need more power to protect my family. You understand that, don't you?"

I closed my eyes. "Yes. I understand."

"Do you?" His voice wrapped me in velvety folds. "I am glad you've come here. I have so much to give you, Rosalind. Rest. Safety. And so much more. But you must give me a boon." His voice whispered in my mind. *What will you give me?*

I hesitated only a moment. Ragnar's face flashed before me. Then Loki's.

I reached into my bodice and drew out the dagger in its sheath. So small. A lady's weapon.

The moonstone flared bright.

"How lovely." The Corpse King reached out a hand. Long, elegant fingers. Skin so pale, never touched by the sun.

I laid the dagger in his palm.

"Thank you, Rosalind." He closed his long fingers around it, his grasp swallowing the light. "Welcome to your new home."

* * *

Loki

"I CAN'T BELIEVE she ran from me." I ducked under a dead tree limb, grimacing as my sleeve caught on some thorns.

The wolf at my side barked.

"Oh, I can believe that she ran from you," I said to Wolf Ragnar. "That was her plan all along. But the witches told her to stay with me."

I waved a hand at the briars blocking our path. They were

so brittle and dry, one puff of magical air from my palm, and they disintegrated.

"Would that I had all of my powers," I muttered. The wolf pushed past me his thick coat impervious to the thorns. I followed him. Ahead stretched what looked like a beautiful forest. But as soon as we grew close, the beauty proved an illusion. The lush trees turned into a dusty wilderness. A stream ran alongside us, yellow and brackish.

"It's not entirely her fault," I mused aloud. "She has been abused and neglected most of her life. God knows what happened to her at that orphanage." Black thorns snagged my breeches and I gritted my teeth, ripping my leg away. "Anyway," I huffed as I caught up with the wolf. "That is why she is prickly."

The wolf snorted.

"Arrogant," I continued. "Slow to trust. Difficult to know."

The wolf put on a burst of speed. I strode to catch up with him.

"The angry ones are filled with hidden pain," I called. "The ones who wear the thickest armor, hurt the most. It's exhausting, though. You never feel safe. You can never let your guard down for anyone…"

The wolf stopped in his tracks and turned his head to regard me with glowing yellow eyes.

"I'm not talking about myself." I laid a hand on my chest. "I'm talking about Rosalind."

The wolf lowered his head, chuffed once.

"We need to be patient with her, that's all I'm saying." This time, I pushed past the wolf. A few more strides, and the mist ahead parted. An obsidian monolith rose before us.

"There you are." I pointed to it. "There's the Corpse King's fortress. That is where we'll find her."

The huge wolf knocked me aside.

"Wait," I snapped. He ignored me, bounding straight towards the open gates. "Ragnar, wait! I know the gates are open but it might be a trap—"

Blue light shot from the tower.

"No!" I threw up my hand, calling on what little power I had. I could not counter the mage's magic, so I used it to shove the wolf out of the way. He sprawled on his side for a second, then sprang onto four paws. He rushed at me, jaws open, teeth long as knives and gleaming and coming closer—

"Odinn's beard!" I tried to dodge. The wolf hit me with his shoulder, and I flew through the air. Magic crackled, exploding the dirt where I'd just been. I hit the ground, and rolled behind a boulder.

The wolf scrambled behind the rock outcropping with me.

"What was that?" I sputtered. I tried to move my shoulder and lost my breath at the searing pain. With a loud crack, my shoulder popped back into place. "You fool," I ranted. "Running ahead, no plan."

The wolf nudged me.

"Don't tell me to shut up. You shut up." I cradled my aching arm and let my head sag against the rock. "You saved my life. Thank you."

You saved mine.

I heard the voice clearly in my head. I turned my head, and met glowing golden eyes.

And then I felt it: a magical surge that washed through me, fizzing through every limb. It opened a window to my mind, laying all my thoughts bare.

The wild beast that was Ragnar stared at me, his golden eyes round and wild.

He felt it too.

What had the witches told me about Berserker magic? It

147

sought to form pack bonds—and further, brother bonds between the warriors so they might survive.

A life for a life. Sacrifice for sacrifice. Such acts of selflessness meant so little when I was a god. But that was all it took to form a brother bond.

Thor's balls. Ragnar's voice spoke straight into my mind.

Thor's balls indeed.

* * *

ROSALIND

"ROSALIND." A ghostly voice calling my name. "Rosalind."

"Loki?"

I was back in the forest, in a glade swathed with mist. I whirled right and left, but didn't see Loki. His mocking voice wrapped around me. "What are you doing, little runaway? Why are you here? Have you given in so easily?"

"No. I am not giving in." I clenched my hands to fists.

Loki emerged from the mist, clad in black like always. Both his eyes were dark. "Do you not remember?"

He touched his fingers to my head, and I saw myself standing before the Corpse King. Only he did not look like a young man, but a horrible half skeleton, wrapped in grave clothes. *Wait for me, my bride,* the mage had said. He'd touched his bony fingers to my forehead, and I'd fallen into a trance.

"This is a dream," I told Loki, and shivered.

"Yes. The mage's power cannot reach us here." He shrugged off his black cloak and wrapped me in it. I ran a hand over the soft folds, savoring the warmth from his body, even if it was all in my head. "You cannot hide here forever, Rosalind. You must face him."

"No," I cried out as I remembered fully, and covered my face with my hands. "It's too late. I gave him the dagger. He has the moonstone." I clenched my teeth, hating to speak of the horror. "I gave it to him willingly."

"Poor Rosalind. He entranced you. But all is not lost. I am here." Loki's fingers tugged mine away. He stroked my face. "There have been some... complications. But I came as soon as I could."

"You've come to save me then." My voice contained my old sarcasm.

"Don't look so shocked," he whispered back with a sharp-edged smile. "This time, I will be a hero."

"How?" Our faces were so close, our breath mingled.

In answer, he slanted his head and brushed his lips against mine. He was so warm, and I was so cold. Cold as if I'd been turned to stone. A mere touch of Loki's lips sent life-giving heat through me. I sighed as if waking from a long sleep.

"Yes," he murmured. "Let me remind you who you are."

His kiss was slow. It set my blood simmering. My heart beat once more. I raised my hand, and cupped his fine cheek. I could feel again.

"What did the Corpse King tell you, Rosalind?" Loki pulled away to stroke my hair back. "What did he promise you?"

"He said I would be his bride."

"Did he now?"

"He said I belong to him."

"We can't have that." He cupped my face. His fingers were long and elegant, but warm. "I will lay my own claim on you." His mouth slanted across mine, his stubble scraping my face as he drank deeply, stroking his tongue into my mouth until I felt his magic touch between my sex.

"A kiss," he hummed, "my most favorite weapon." He kept sipping sweetness from my lips, as if I were the finest mead.

I pressed myself to him, needing him as he needed me. His taste was ambrosia, rich and heavy. His sharp winter-green scent surrounded me, cleansing my senses. "You broke the spell."

A corner of his mouth turned down. "It will not last. When you awaken, you will still be in his thrall."

I laid a hand on his chest, seeking his heartbeat with my palm. "You did your best. Loki, I..." I sought the words but they seemed so small considering the enormity of what I felt. "I am glad you're here," I said awkwardly. "Even if it is only a dream."

He chuckled and tucked me close, wrapping his cloak about both of us. "Look at the two of us. Carefully guarding our hearts so nothing will break them. Cutting them off from light and air, not caring if they wither, because we think it is safe. It doesn't work, Rosalind." He nuzzled my head. "In the end, it makes us brittle. And we will shatter."

My lips had frozen again. "I am already broken."

He pressed a kiss to my head. "We are all broken. There is no shame in it. Between the three of us, we make one whole."

"Three of us?"

"Mmm." He sounded resigned.

Rosalind, someone in the distance bellowed. The sound twisted into a wolf's howl. Something was lurking in the forest. Half man, half beast, all monster.

"Don't you know never to feed wild animals?" Loki mused. "You gave that feral oaf a piece of your heart. Now we can't get rid of him."

"I must go to him." I tried to pull away, but Loki tugged me back.

"He's been insufferable since you ran off. I can't promise he won't make you regret it."

Another painful bellow. The ache in the sound tore my heart.

"Let me go to him. Loki, please."

"He doesn't want to see you, I'm afraid. Not in his current form."

Beyond the mist came a broken, snuffling sound. The monster's breathing.

"Ragnar," I called, and the heavy breathing came closer.

I pushed away from Loki, heading towards the sound. I stopped just short of the swirling mist. "Come closer," I called.

Loki stepped to my side. "As I said, he doesn't want to see you."

A snarl came from the shadows.

"He says he's a monster," Loki translated.

"I want you, Ragnar. If you are a monster, then that is how I want you." The wind picked up and I raised my voice. "You are not allowed to leave me wanting!"

"You heard the lady," Loki called. To me, he whispered, "It's working, go on."

"Ragnar," I called. "The Corpse King put his mark on me. But you replaced it. I'm in his castle; he says I am to be his bride."

The roar came with a gust of wind that blew my hair back.

"You want to challenge him?" I shouted back. "Come and prove I belong to you."

The mist crept forward. A dark shape moved in the shadows, beyond my sight.

I waved a hand in the thick fog. "This isn't real. This is only a dream."

"Yes, little runaway," Loki murmured at my back, pulling his cloak away, "but it seems you need a reminder of what is real."

A cloth dropped over my eyes. I raised a hand to tug the blindfold away, but Loki tutted and gathered my hands behind me. It was quick and easy work for him to bind them behind my back.

He paused for a moment. "Just go with it," he whispered into my ear. "He needs this."

Ragnar's howl rippled through the night as Loki wrenched me around.

"He'll come for you," Loki said. He marched me forward with his hand clamped on the back of my neck. "Look who I found," he singsonged.

The beast let out a feral purr. I turned my head in its direction but the blindfold held fast.

Loki laughed. "He says perhaps I am not so useless after all."

I wet my lips. "You speak for him?"

Another gusting growl.

"Unfortunately, yes." Loki stepped close, his hands busy above me.

Soon, I was tied up as I was before, with my arms stretched over my head, tethered to a tree branch high above. Were there trees in this magical place?

"Of course," Loki continued. "Neither of us like it."

So much had happened since I ran from them. "How can you understand him?"

"I have many talents." He snapped his fingers, and the air chilled my body. My clothes had fallen away. I twisted naked in the wind.

"What are you doing?" I gasped.

"You know what." Loki's long fingers caressed my bare breast. Despite myself, I arched into his touch. "You've been here before. For once, Ragnar and I agree on something." A howl broke out, melancholy and achingly beautiful. "Do you know what he's saying?"

"No."

"He says you ran from us. Now, you must atone." He gathered my hair and tucked it over my shoulder so it flowed over my breasts, leaving my back bare.. "There. It's time for your punishment."

Even with my arms bound over my head, my toes curled.

"Cold?" Loki stroked my face. "Don't worry. Soon, we will warm you." A whip cracked behind me, making me jump. "We will teach you not to run from us."

"How many?" Ragnar growled behind me, in the voice of the beast.

I tried to twist in his direction, and Loki steadied me.

"As many as she can take." Loki grasped my hips. "Ready, little runaway?"

I braced myself. "Ready."

But there was no way to anticipate Loki lowering his head, his hair brushing my face. His tongue swept inside my mouth, and I melted into him as the first lash hit my back. The strike was a shock to my senses but I felt no pain. The whip cracked again before the echo of the first lash faded from my ears. And then the pain hit me. The sting punched the breath from my lungs. Loki swallowed my cries and then lowered his head to my breast, his teeth gently biting my nipple. He sucked hard.

The whip struck between my shoulder blades again.

Fire blazed a trail between my legs, and Loki slid his hand down my midriff to cup me there. His long fingers probed the petals of my sex, nimbly threading themselves between my labia, gathering the dew that had collected there, and using it to rub along the tender bud that caused little lightning bolts to flash from my sex, burning white hot in my brain.

The lash landed again. I groaned. Loki grasped both my hips. His mouth covered my sex, his tongue licking up my slit, probing there. It found my clit and surrounded it with spiraling circles. He tongued me slowly, as if he had a lifetime to lap at my cunny.

The monster behind me was breathing hard. The whip cracked. My body swayed forward with the impact, but I felt nothing. Instead of pain, I felt a ghostly touch—soft as velvet, light as butterfly wings—dancing over my skin. It flowed up my back in golden rivulets. Everywhere the whip touched, heated velvet followed.

My body arched like a bow. I pressed my sex into Loki's mouth, wishing I could see his face. His hands roamed over my bare chest, sliding up to squeeze one breast and then the other. He played me like a lyre, plucking at my nipples, drawing forth the music of my moans. Pleasure broke over me, tiny golden waves flowing through me, growing larger. This time, when the whip struck, I felt it, and it ignited a golden storm. I cried out, my body tightening as my climax crashed over me. Loki's magic filled my body, pushing out any other sensation until I was made of pure ecstasy.

When I lifted my head, I sensed a presence behind me. Loki was still on his knees before me, toying with my sex. His hair brushed my belly.

But behind me lurked a giant. Prickles ran up my back, warning me that a predator was close. Hot breath puffed onto my neck. I sensed the creature was bigger and taller than anything I'd ever encountered. A monster.

Ragnar.

"Cut her down," it growled. A thrill of fear ran through me, transmuted to pleasure by some wicked alchemy of Loki's magic.

Loki released my hips. "Are you sure?"

Ragnar didn't answer, and Loki's sigh gusted against my bare flesh.

"Very well." He rose.

There was a *snick* as the knife parted the leather thong holding me up. My arms dropped.

Ragnar growled. "Run."

I staggered forward, stumbling as I found my footing. As soon as I did, I dashed forward. My fingers tore at the blindfold, ripping it off. But it did no good. All around me was mist.

I raced into the night.

A growl filled the world, so loud, the ground shook. Fear stabbed me, spurring me forward. I became a rabbit, white-eyed and dashing away from the wolf snapping at its heels. Only there wasn't one monster chasing me. A shape loomed in the shadows next to me, and I veered to the right. The beast behind me gained speed, coming up on my left. I change directions again. The two monsters herded me between them until at last, one pounced. I lost my footing and rolled. The furred bulk of the monster covered me, catching me mid fall, and lowering me to the ground before pinning me down.

I lay covered in a blanket of cedar-scented fur. The black shape loomed over me. Fur crackled down his strong forearms. I struggled, and his eyes flashed gold. He lowered his wolf's head and covered my shoulder with his huge mouth. Long white canines pressed into my skin without breaking it.

"Ragnar," I panted. His ears twitched forward.

I raised a hand and stroked the fur on the monster's face. His teeth left my skin. Hot breath caressed my face. For a moment, his heavy, heated weight pressed me into the forest floor. Then he moved off me and flipped me to my hands and knees. Something hot and thick rubbed the back of my leg, smearing fluid. I braced myself on my forearms, tipping forward to offer up my sex. And then I held very still.

Heavy paws grasped my hips, pulling me back. A cock,

long and thick as a tree branch, rubbed between my legs. Fur chafed my backside. The dagger-sharp tips of the monster's claws bit into my thighs.

"Yes," I whispered. "Do it."

The beast rumbled, and thrust inside. I cried out, shuddering forward. I felt his length and girth down to my toes. He was too big. Claws scraped my skin. The beast that was Ragnar filled me.

A second black shape blocked out the moonlight. Another furred monster, this one with raven-black eyes.

"Rosalind," he purred in Loki's voice. I closed my eyes. A large hand grasped my hair, claws scratching lightly at my scalp. A cock touched my lips. I licked the tip, tasting salt and intoxicating sweetness. I closed my mouth over it. The taste and scent of Loki surrounded me. I sucked greedily, wanting more.

"Take it." His voice thickened. His cock pushed deeper. I dug my fingers into the earth, willing myself to open. To accept more of them.

"That's it," Loki hissed. "That's the way."

Behind me, Ragnar rocked slowly, inching deeper into my sex. I was so full. My belly cramped, but my inner muscles clenched, rippling over Ragnar's cock. My cunny was greedy for more.

Then, inexplicably, Ragnar withdrew. Loki tugged my hair, pulling my mouth from his cock.

I whined, and Loki laughed. "Patience." He lifted me in his furred arms, settling me on his cock. I was already stretched from Ragnar's rod. Loki entered easily, but he was longer. I groaned as he slid deep—groaned, then shuddered.

"She's ready," Loki muttered.

A clawed hand collared my throat, tipping me back. "Open for me," Ragnar purred. His cock nudged my rear, pushing between my bottom cheeks. The wet leaking from his cock painted my arsehole, and then he was pushing inside. My tiny opening resisted. Ragnar's growl rumbled through me. Slowly, ever so slowly, the blunt head of his cock stretched me.

"Too much," I moaned. "Too full."

"You can take it." Loki bent over me, licking at my lips. Fangs brushed my face.

"You will take it," Ragnar rumbled.

My fingers flexed, gripping the silky folds of Loki's fur. I reached back and touched the furred bulk that was Ragnar.

"Mine." Ragnar's fangs grazed my shoulder as if he might carve the words into my flesh. "Mine."

Together, the monsters rocked deeper inside me. I shuddered in their hold.

Somehow, my body stretched to accommodate them. Deep inside me, the two cocks rubbed my inner channels, stimulating every part of me. They thrust in tandem, rocking in and out of me, stretching me further. I felt like I was breaking apart.

But then my clit caught a furred ridge. The motion of Loki's thrusts rubbed the right parts of me, and the sting of the stretch transformed into something sweeter.

A burst of light grew in my belly. I was no longer made of flesh, but golden sensation.

Teeth fastened onto my shoulder, and I exploded. Light blazed through me.

Both monsters roared, impaling me on their stiffened rods. Wet heat seared my insides.

Loki pulled out, but Ragnar kept pumping in my ass, filling me so full, I felt that if I opened my mouth, his seed might spurt out of me.

I shuddered, limp. Ragnar slid his paw from my neck and

steadied me against him as he slid out. Against my back, his chest rumbled with something like a purr.

They rolled me to a resting place between them. Their cedar and wintergreen scents blended over me. They were still monsters, but I didn't care. They were my monsters.

The stars swirled overhead. I was dissolving into them, becoming bigger than myself. Someone safe and secure and more powerful. I reached up to touch the sky and for a moment, I was made of more than just flesh. I caught a glimpse of a woman who looked just like me. Her hair was the stuff of stars. Her eyes contained worlds. She was everything I wanted, everything I wished to be. One glimpse, and she was gone.

She's not gone. She's inside you. Loki spoke into my mind. *You can find her again, and call upon her at will.*

"The mage is waiting for me. I must go back."

It does not matter. Ragnar's voice echoed in my head. *You will always be ours.*

I touched the puncture wounds at the juncture of my shoulder and neck. "Will this be enough to claim me?"

No, little runaway. There's more to come, and you must be brave. But we will be by your side.

"But how?" I asked aloud.

We will not abandon you, Ragnar rasped. *Nothing will stop us from coming to you.*

A wrenching pain caught me unawares. I cried out. The Corpse King's magic was upon me, and I could not escape.

"He's pulling me back," I gasped. "It hurts." But as soon as I said that, the numbness spread over me—my body turning to stone once more.

Wait for us, Ragnar growled. *Promise me.*

"Promise." I touched his face, wishing I could imprint the memory of him on my fingers. He nipped my fingers, and I welcomed the red burst of pain. I'd take the pain, so long as I could still feel.

Fear not, Loki said as the mage's spell overtook me, surrounding me in darkness. I saw nothing, felt nothing, but their voices lingered, and I clung to their promise.

We will come for you.

CHAPTER 10

WHEN I WOKE, I knew it had only been a moment, and yet I stood in the great hall. I wore a fine gown that looked like it was made of spun silver. Lovely, fit for a queen.

"You wish for me to be your bride." My frozen lips shaped the words.

"Yes," said the mage. He was standing behind me. "I need sons. I will fill the world with them. I will rule with you." His spidery fingers stroked over my midriff as if trying to caress my womb.

"Without me, you have no power then. Why should I give up my power for you?"

"Sweet Rosalind. You've already succumbed."

It was true. My limbs were frozen as if I was wrapped in cobwebs. How could I fight him?

A sound interrupted us then. A frantic howling.

"What is that?" I turned my head to the sound. It seemed familiar, somehow.

The mage gave a frustrated grunt. "My magic has ensnared two creatures outside the castle."

"What creatures?" My voice echoed, sounding other-worldly.

"Two wolves. Wretched beasts."

"Show me?"

A creaking sigh, and the mage snapped his fingers. Two wolves—one black, one brown and grey, both smeared with dust and soot—strained towards us.

"They are not just wolves," I said, catching glimpses of men trapped inside. "They are cursed." Somehow, I could see the magic on them. A tightening black net.

"Poor souls," the mage said. "Shall I free them?"

I nodded, he flung out a hand. The wolves whined, twisting in some invisible grip. He was hurting them.

"Wait!" I reached out to him. "My lord, please wait. I would have these beasts be spared. Give them to me."

The mage's hand closed into a fist. "They cannot be tamed."

"Then let them be leashed. Please. I will marry you will-ingly. Give me their lives as a wedding gift."

The mage lowered his hand. "A wedding gift then."

I was already crossing the hall to approach them. They stood panting, the mage's magic leashing them.

"Don't be scared." I held out a hand to the nearest one.

For a moment, it stood still, letting me approach. Then it lunged. The wolf's teeth caught my flesh. The fangs sank in deep into the top of my hand, almost piercing it straight through. I cried out.

Then blue light struck the wolf's side, flinging the crea-ture away. It hit a column and yelped once. Its limp body slid to the base. The other wolf rose up, running to sniff and lick at its fallen comrade.

"Filthy beast," the mage said without much emotion in his voice. "Did it hurt you?"

I held my hand to my breast it throbbed wildly. I couldn't keep my eyes off the wolf.

"No," I managed, even though the pain rose up bright and blossoming in my head. "It does not hurt much."

I blinked. It was as if a veil had been peeled back from my sight. And now I saw things as they were.

This palatial hall was not grand or beautiful. It was close, and dark as a cave. The fine columns were really stalactites, dripping water. Spiders scuttled around, spinning their webs in every corner.

And the Corpse King next to me... oh, he was a monster worse than a Berserker. Tall and skeletal, with skin receding from the shining bone of his skull and face. His skin was grey. Grave clothes wound about his limbs and chest. He wore grand robes that were dull and dusty with age. He was not in his full power.

Everything he had shown me, everything he had spun, was a lie. And now I could see clearly.

The wolf that was Loki lay in a broken heap beside the wall of the cave. The wolf that was Ragnar licked the fallen wolf's face, and let out a low whine. Loki's bite had broken the spell. He had sacrificed so I might see.

Rosalind, Ragnar's voice spoke directly into my head.

I startled. For a second, I hesitated, frozen. Then I opened my heart and let the rush of Ragnar's hopes and fears, love and connection rush in. *I'm here. Is Loki...?*

The wolf whined again. *I cannot reach him.*

"Shall I dispose of the body?" the mage was asking me.

"No. Bear him outside and lay him out at the foot of a tree," I said. *Go with him,* I told Ragnar. *I will be safe.*

A magic wind lifted the limp body, bearing it from the hall. The brown and white wolf turned glowing eyes to me.

Please. I stretched out a hand by my side, and spread my fingers. *Make sure he is safe.*

Wolf Ragnar's ears flattened to his head.

The mage flicked his fingers and a burst of wind hit the wolf, pushing him back.

Go now, I ordered. *Save your strength. There is nothing you can do here.*

I will return, Ragnar the wolf promised. *Wait for me.*

I promise. Relief turned my joints to liquid when the wolf turned and left.

"That is the way when you keep wild animals." The Corpse King shrugged. "Now, my dear. Shall we?" He extended his hand to me. I stared at his skeletal fingers. They were little more than animated bones.

Beyond him shimmered several thin plumes of smoke. Silvery blue and glowing, they looked like the ghostly will-o'-the-wisp that hovered over the marshes.

As I stared, the mist solidified into the shapes of women. They stood in a row, all manner of heights and sizes. I could make them out clearly. There was a round woman with honey gold hair spilling across her shoulders. Beside her stood a taller woman, with hollowed cheeks and dark, slanting eyes. She shook her head solemnly. The blonde woman shook her head more vigorously. *No,* she mouthed to me. *No.*

They did not want me to take his hand. My instincts were right. If I touched him, I might fall under his spell again.

I would not let Loki's sacrifice be in vain.

Please be well, I prayed silently, hoping somehow Loki could hear me.

"Rosalind." The Corpse King was waiting.

"Please." I used both my hands to pick up my skirts. They

weren't silvery at all, but covered in dust and cobwebs. I hid my shudder. I'd rather touch the remains of spiders than the Corpse King's hand. "Lead the way," I said. I did not want to touch him lest his veil drop over my sight again.

He nodded, though he looked displeased. "Then come." His cape swept along the cobwebbed floor. At his hip, the moonstone winked its jeweled eye at me. I had to find a way to get the dagger back, and thrust it into the mage's heart.

The mage led me to the end of the hall and up three stairs onto a raised dais.

The flock of ghostly woman had followed us. They stood huddled in the corner, the eerie blue light shaping their bodies shimmering. They were here to guide me.

But the Corpse King had so much power. How could I fight him? One touch, and he might veil my mind.

"Here." The mage approached a grand table, and pulled out a chair. "Let us dine."

Both table and chairs were made of stone. The table was set with what once might have been fine dishes that were now cracked and filled with cobwebs. There was something that might have been fruit in a bowl, now rotten and putrefied into sludge.

I swallowed my bile, and took the seat the mage offered, careful not to touch him. If he bespelled me again, I did not know how I'd get free.

"Drink." The mage filled a goblet with a thick red liquid. I took it, fighting the urge to hold my nose and gag. I had to act like I was still under the spell, and pretend the liquid was red wine even though it was nothing of the sort. Under the clove and incense scent of the mage's magic, the rusty tang of blood was strong.

I raised the goblet in a toast. "To power," I said. My voice echoed oddly around the cobwebbed hall.

"Power." He nodded, and sipped. I watched in fascination as more flesh crawled, knitting over the exposed bone of his bald head. His features would be like that of the young man's when his magic was done remaking him.

"What vintage is this?" I asked, pretending to drink.

"From my old lands," he said. "The blood of my sons made it possible."

I gritted my teeth against the urge to gag. I set down the goblet, my hand shaking with the urge to throw it from me.

"My sons... they have all perished now." The mage sounded almost sad.

I looked past him to the women clustered beyond his shoulder. "And their mothers? Your wives?"

"They were unworthy of me," he said. "At the last, they abandoned me. Turned against me. I have been alone so long." The look in his eye chilled me. "I need a queen to rule by my side."

A spider scuttled down the table, disappearing between the dishes.

"Are you full?" the mage asked.

I looked down at the rotted substance in the bowl in front of me. I could not bring myself to pretend to eat any longer. "Quite," I managed.

"Then let us begin." He swept out a hand, and a magic wind pushed the dishes aside. Now I saw the stone table for what it was.

An altar. A stone slab, stained with brown. The stains were not spilled wine, but blood. The blood of his sons, of his wives. The Corpse King had sacrificed them for more power, and he would sacrifice me.

"You want power, too," he observed. "Come, Rosalind, and I will give it to you."

Something in me surged. I did want power. But not at this price.

In my mind, I reached for Ragnar. *Don't let me slip away*, I whispered, and an answer echoed in my head.

We won't. Two voices. Loki and Ragnar's, blended together. For a moment, I inhaled both a wintergreen and a cedar scent.

Had Loki survived?

"Join with me," the Corpse King continued. "I will give you a crown." He raised his hands, and fashioned one out of the air with magic. But when it appeared, it was made of old bones.

I swallowed.

The mage set the construct on my hair before I could protest. I closed my eyes. I could smell the decay.

"Too long, we've tarried," the mage intoned. He lifted me and laid me down on the stained table. He loomed over me, and I averted my head. I stretched out my hand and brushed the mage's hip where he wore the dagger. The blade was under my fingers but I could not free it.

My fingers brushed the moonstone. *The moonstone is the weapon*, the witches had said. *It is the source of power and can be used to bind him.*

The surface of the moonstone was smooth under my fingertips.

You have an affinity for it, Loki had said. *You have magic.*

I rubbed the stone. The mage's breath was fetid on my face.

Come to me, I called to the moonstone. At my thought, the gem slipped free. I fumbled it between my fingers. I was not as deft as Loki, but could do his trick well enough because he had taught me.

Well done, Loki's voice echoed in my head.

Help me, I whispered back. I had the moonstone, but what now?

Behind my head, there was a sudden clatter. The mage

drew back, and for a moment, I could breathe again.

"What was that?" I asked.

The mage's skull-like head lit a moment with blue light, and then he opened his mouth and belched magic. I felt something snuff out, and the hall went silent.

My eyes watered in the thickly perfumed air. The mage had cast some great spell, and now I felt the aftermath of his oppressive magic like a weight on my chest, making it difficult to breathe.

"My dead wives mock me," he muttered.

I craned my head. The ghostly figures in the hall were gone, leaving only sinister darkness.

In my head, Ragnar was roaring. The sound blended with a clearer, louder roar.

The mage whirled, his cloak swirling.

The castle shook. Stones and spiders rained down. I cried out, and covered my face. Outside the hall doors came shouts and more roars.

"The Berserkers have come." The mage's voice was a hollow boom, ringing in my aching ears. "They are attacking."

I pushed myself up off the altar, and the mage turned on me.

"I need power." He slammed me down. Bones crunched in my shoulder, and pain knifed through me. I pressed my lips together to keep from crying out.

I'd slipped the stone into my mouth. Its smooth weight rested on my tongue.

"It is too late." The mage tempered his voice. "They will not be able to stand against us, my Queen."

I knew it was true. I needed to bind him to the moonstone.

With my good arm, I gripped his shoulder, drawing him forward.

The mage gave a horrible chuckle, and bent his shining bald head to mine.

A kiss, Loki had said, *is a most dangerous thing.*

I reared up at the last, and thrust my tongue into the Corpse King's mouth, pushing the moonstone down his throat. I kept my mouth pressed against his, gagging against the stench.

You have power, Rosalind. You had it all along.

Go! I willed the moonstone to take on a life of its own. I imagined it wriggling down the mage's throat, choking him.

For a moment, nothing happed. The mage seized me, tossing me from the table. I hit the wretched stones, and pain punched me. I lay, shuddering, unable to move.

Above me, the Corpse King staggered, his skeletal fingers gripping the table. Blue light burst from his eye sockets and the gaps in his graveclothes. The moonstone illuminated the browned bones underneath.

A blast of magic shook the castle, emanating from the Corpse King's form. Larger stones tumbled down. I curled up as best I could, ignoring the spiders scuttling over me. They were fleeing for their lives. In vain. This place was made with the Corpse King's power, and with the moonstone binding his power, it was collapsing.

The witches are here. Ragnar's voice came to me. *They are chanting outside the gates.* He pushed an image into my mind: a circle of black-clad women, the outer ring holding hands. A few crones knelt in the center, writing runes. Standing in the middle of the circle was a blonde woman with pale arms stretched to the sky. Her eyes were black.

They were using the moonstone as a focal point to bind the mage.

It's working. I sent back an image of the Corpse King. He was standing rigid, his arms locked to his sides. Then the castle shuddered, and a fall of stone blocked my view of him.

The Berserkers are tearing the tower apart. I saw with Ragnar's eyes what was going on outside. A long line of warriors hammered axes against the obsidian sides of the mage's construct. Cracks appeared in the bespelled walls. A few furred monsters clawed at the cracks, fishing out pieces of magic-made stone and hurling them aside.

You did it, Rosalind. You've won. Ragnar's voice was tinged with fear. *Now you must flee!*

I cannot. At my feet, a stone pinned my gown. I tried to rise, and agony bloomed in my head. My vision blackened.

No! Ragnar roared. *This cannot be the end!*

I always knew I would die. That is what was prophesied.

No!

Go, Ragnar. Free yourself.

Blue smoke flickered in the corner of my eye. I turned my head slowly. The ghostly figures in the corner were there again. But this time, they were more solid. Everything, from the shadows on their faces to the weave of their woolen cloaks, looked more real. Whatever the Corpse King had done to banish his former brides hadn't lasted long.

Two of them knelt beside me.

Go, daughter, they said. Their ghostly hands reached out, and the rock on my gown tumbled away. A cold hand landed on my shoulder, freezing the pain for a moment. Another at my back pushed me up, steadying me until I found my feet. A ghostly face flashed in front of me. The round cheeked blonde woman. *Go now.* She touched my face and strength flowed into me. I stumbled, making my way around a pile of rocks.

My body felt full of cobwebs.

The roars outside were getting louder. Light began to break in. The tower was being torn apart. Soon, the structure would fall.

"Rosalind," a voice hissed behind me. Black lines of power snaked around me, tugging me back.

The spectral women surged around me. Ghostly hands gripped the lines, pulling them off. But there were so many.

Despair leaked through me. The Corpse King stood in a blue glow. He stretched out his hand, and pointed at my forehead. *Die.*

I threw up my hands, but they were no match for the magic knifing through me. The faces of the ghostly women flashed before my eyes as I fell backwards.

Wait, the round-cheeked one mouthed to me. She pointed towards the side of the tower where a dark shape emerged from the rubble, its golden eyes wild.

Ragnar. He came for me, as promised.

Rosalind! The monster grabbed me, clutching my broken body to his furred chest. Pain wracked me, and I cried out feebly.

The beast roared, bending over to protect me from the falling obsidian shards. The movement wracked my body. Darkness closed its jaws around me. As I lost my grip on consciousness, Ragnar's promise followed me down.

I will not let you die.

* * *

Ragnar

ROSALIND LAY limp in my arms. I cradled her to my chest, hunching over as rubble rained upon my back. Ahead, light streamed through the cracks in the tower's side. The whole structure shuddered. I dashed over the fallen rocks, my claws tearing as I fought my way forward. A stone fell from the ceiling and smashed my side. I let out a roar.

This will not be how it ends!

Ghostly light flashed around me. A woman's face appeared at my side, her mouth open in a silent shout. I startled back but she grabbed my arm and hoisted me onward. Blue light glimmered overhead, and stones bounced off the protective bubble.

I hit the side of the tower and burst forth with a roar. Berserkers ranged along the tower's sides, hacking it apart with their axes. Monsters as big as me ripped at the stones with their bare paws.

A hundred yards back, beside a grove of half-dead trees, a knot of four Berserkers in ancient armor stood around the circle of witches, protecting them.

I bounded towards the treeline, shaking my head to clear the blood from my eyes. My side itched but the wounds were already knitting together.

Rosalind, the beast raged in my breast. I strode to the shade of an old, gnarled oak. At the trunk's base lay Loki's body. The wily bastard looked serene, as if he was not dead, merely in repose.

When I laid Rosalind down beside him, he opened his eyes. "You got her out." He coughed. "Well done."

So, you're not dead. I spoke to him with my mind.

The right corner of his mouth tugged up. *Not yet.* He sounded disappointed. His hand fluttered at his side. His black jerkin was wet. He touched it, and his fingers came away smeared red. "Mortal bodies are so frail," he observed.

You're a Berserker, I replied. *You should heal.*

"Not from this. It was a death curse." He let his head sag back, rolling it to the side to observe Rosalind. "There is one upon her, as well. She is dying."

No! I roared. With a gentle claw, I brushed golden hair back from Rosalind's face. She was so beautiful, regal even in repose.

"The witches," Loki rasped. "Get them. There might be something they can do."

I rose, lurching as the ground shook.

Back by the tower, draugr had risen. The tide of Berserkers turned to fight them. Warriors swung axes, snarling and howling.

The witches now thronged the remains of the tower with their hands outstretched. A blue light shot up from the pile of rubble. The women's hair blasted back in an invisible wind. A loud moaning rose from the rocky pile. Witches screamed, and Berserkers roared.

Light flashed and I hunched, shielding my eyes.

The earth shook. I raced back on all fours to Rosalind, hunching over her.

Then all at once, the world was silent.

I straightened, pawing Rosalind's pale cheek. *Wait for me, Rosalind. You promised.*

Then I ran for the witches.

* * *

Loki

THOR'S HAIRY BALLS, the death curse hurt.

"This is what comes of being a hero," I muttered. My hand pressed my side, as if it would do a bit of good. My slowly healing wounds were not going to kill me. The black net of magic around my heart, would.

Hurry up, Ragnar.

I'm trying, he growled back. Charming as ever.

I closed my eyes and merged my mind with Ragnar's so I could see what he saw.

"The Corpse King is bound," said one of the witches with

a long, hawk-like nose. Four warriors thronged her—her mates. The largest touched his temple and when his fingers came away red, he grinned and licked the blood from his hand.

"We will stand guard," Yseult said, and her mates nodded. "He will not stir for another thousand years."

Ragnar roared and the four warriors snapped into formation, shielding their mate from his attack.

"He has gone mad," one growled.

"Oh no," I croaked. "This is not good."

"Wait," a musical voice called. A young witch threw herself between Ragnar and the four armed warriors. Her dark hair blew around her face and her chest heaved as if she'd run a mile. She wore the black rags of an ancient crone, but her face was young.

"He is not mad. His mate is hurt." She held up a hand, and faced Ragnar. "Show me."

She strode behind him, her black-clad sisters following.

Soon, they were all standing over Rosalind and me.

The dark-haired young woman sank to her knees between us.

"Rosalind." Her fingers stroked the still face. "You have saved us all."

Ragnar pushed closer, growling.

"No, I cannot heal her," the witch answered him. "She is too far gone."

The monster that was Ragnar fell to his knees.

Brother, I mouthed. I stretched out my fingers, wanting to comfort him.

"Ah." The dark-haired witch turned her black eyes to me. "There is another wounded here. Shall we see what we can do for him?" She leaned close, and I had a burst of Seeing.

"I know you." I crooked a brow at the young witch. She shot me a dazzling smile.

"Give me my staff." She motioned without taking her raven-black eyes from mine. Someone handed her the staff and her image rippled, revealing the crone.

I blinked, and she was not a crone, but beautiful, with shining black hair and smooth cheeks. "Loki Laufeyjarson."

"I am dying." I flopped my hand to my chest. "Mourn me forever."

"Such dramatics," the witch tsked. "We will not mourn you at all."

I pouted. "I'm hurt."

"No need to mourn if you survive." The witch's black eyes twinkled, and she raised her voice. "Sisters. Has he fulfilled the bargain? Shall we tell Odinn what he's done?"

"But what is it I'm supposed to have done?"

"You learned your lesson. Sacrificed yourself for another."

"No," I murmured and turned my head to face Rosalind's still form. "I failed. I was supposed to keep her safe."

"So. Keep her then." The beautiful woman who was also the crone waved a hand and disappeared. Above, on a branch, a raven squawked.

A searing light hit me, sizzling through my body. The pain of my wounds was nothing compared to this agony.

Someone was shouting. I wished they would shut up, the sound pierced my ears.

After a moment, I realized that the one shouting was me.

* * *

Ragnar

WHAT IS HAPPENING, I growled to the Berserkers behind the witches. *What have they done?*

"They petitioned Odinn for that one's power," the

Berserkers' mate, Yseult, replied, nodding to Loki. The four Berserkers removed their bronze helmets, their golden eyes on the fallen warrior's body. Loki jerked, going rigid. His teeth were bared in a grimace. Lightning flashed, striking the ground around him.

A loud shout rang out, and Loki shot to his feet. Both his eyes were black as a raven's.

My fur stood on end.

Loki closed his mouth, and the shouting stopped. He stared at his hands a moment. "Yes," he breathed. "Odinn's beard. I'm back!"

Brother, I choked out. We were still linked, mind to mind. Power throbbed on Loki's end of the bond, a blazing ball of light.

"Finally." Loki opened his hands, and fireballs danced on his palms. A cloak unfurled from his shoulders. He turned, and a thunderclap cracked overhead.

"Shut up, Thor," Loki muttered. He waved to the witches. "Stand back." The women scurried out of his way—all except for the dark-haired one, who leaned on her staff.

"It's too late," she croaked. "Rosalind is dead. It was foretold."

"Never mind that." Loki stalked forward, his gaze intent on Rosalind's face. "Give her to me."

"It's too late," the witch insisted.

"For a man." Loki set his hands on her shoulders and pushed her gently aside. "Not for a god."

He knelt at Rosalind's side and gathered her into his arms. Her head lolled on his shoulder.

He turned, and searched the somber faces until he found mine. He winked at me, and raised his head to the sky. Between one breath and the next, he and Rosalind disappeared.

 osalind

COOL AIR WAFTED over my face. There was a blast of wintergreen scent, and long fingers were stroking over my brow.

"Rosalind," Loki murmured.

I let my eyes crack open. "Did we win?"

"Yes."

"Am I dying?"

"I believe you already did. As was foretold."

My eyes flew open. "Where are we?" Light danced overhead, filtering through a gold and green canopy of leaves.

"Somewhere death cannot touch us." Loki's grin was smug. He looked the same, yet different somehow. His black hair was a little longer. Both his eyes were black.

I swallowed. "Did you die?"

"Almost," he replied cheerfully. "The witches petitioned Odinn. It seems my deeds were found worthy. I have my power back. See?" He passed a hand over my face and warmth spread over my body.

My chest ached as if my bodice was too tight. I struggled to draw a breath, but the rest of my body was blissfully numb.

"Here." Loki helped me sit up.

I was also much changed. My dress was different—a rich blue. The fabric shimmered in the light.

"To match your eyes." He tucked a strand of my hair behind my ear. "Did you know, Rosalind, your eyes glow like magic moonstones in the night?"

"No," I answered, absently fiddling with my hair. The shining tresses were clean and cobweb free. I shuddered, remembering the spiders.

Loki scooted closer. "How do you feel?"

I laid a hand on my chest. "Better. What is this place?" Huge trees surrounded the glade, their trunks wider than any I'd ever seen. I lay on a bed of thick moss.

"A sanctuary. You've been here before. I brought you here when you were in the Corpse King's thrall. Only spirits can reside here. Spirits, and the dead."

"Oh." I was dead. No wonder I felt numb.

"Your quest is over," Loki said gently. "You can go to your deserved rest. Or…"

"Or?"

"Or… I can perform one last trick." Loki glanced around, ducked his head close and whispered, "How would you like to be reborn?"

There was magic on his minty breath. Goosebumps peppered my arms. "What do you mean?"

He blinked, and both his eyes were green and earnest on mine. He crouched closer. "Tell me, Rosalind… do you want to die?"

I thought of my sister, and the spaewives on Berserker Mountain. They were safe now, because of what I had done.

I did not need to return for them.

But then I thought of Ragnar. The blond warrior, roaring. Dogging my steps. Fighting to fulfill his promises to me.

Perhaps it was not too late. Perhaps I could choose to return... for me.

"No," I murmured. "I want to live."

"Good girl." Loki leaned forward ,and pressed his lips to my forehead.

"But what about the prophecy?"

"The prophecy has been fulfilled. You did die. Just enough to be reborn."

A snap of his fingers, and the tight web around my chest eased. A coughing spell took me, making me bend in half. When I wiped my mouth, red foam flecked my fingers.

"Enough of that," Loki boomed, and his face shone with a godly light. He splayed a hand on my chest and sent his power surging through me. It hurt like he was unmaking me.

I cried out.

"The death curse is strong," Loki said, calmly. "But I can make you stronger." His eyes blazed black once more. "Tell me, Rosalind. Do you want power?"

Light danced along his fingertips. He pressed them to my face. Lightning shot through my body. Every nerve shrieked.

I opened my mouth, and screamed. Even as I writhed, warmth spread through me, followed by a cool, tingling feeling. The sensation pushed through me until I was full, and there was no room for my organs or bones.

All at once, the pain was gone. My insides felt new. Power rippled through me. Loki was no longer touching me—the power was mine, and mine alone. I felt it brimming in me, an endless well of light.

I licked my lips. "What have you done to me?"

His eyes were black again. "Awakened your magic. Lent you a little of mine. Did you know that a goddess resides in you? I might have let her out."

I stared at my hands. When I moved my arms, my skin rippled, and I caught a glimpse of starlight.

Loki sprawled out next to me. "How do you feel?"

"Strange."

"You'll get used to it."

I touched my lips. My face and form were unblemished. Energy surged through me, and power followed, ready to come at my call. "Did I truly die?"

"Yes. You'll get used to that, too. Now..." He rubbed his hands together. "We seem to be missing someone."

He snapped his fingers, and a circle of light appeared. It widened until it was larger than a man. There was a roar, and a dark shape crashed through.

Rosalind!

I rose. Power flashed through my legs, strengthening them even as I moved. The sensation was strange. I took my first step as a reborn creature, wobbly as a new colt. *Ragnar.*

The monster hesitated.

Come. I motioned, and he crossed the remaining feet to crouch before me. I laid my hands on his cheeks, my fingers sliding into the fur. Almost immediately, the fur and features of the beast melted away until Ragnar the man stood before me. He rose and stretched, rubbing his arms, newly free of fur.

Well done, Loki spoke into my mind. *Goddess, you use your powers well.*

I ignored him. Things were too strange.

"Rosalind," Ragnar rasped, taking my hand. "You are much changed."

"Whereas you have remained the same." I raised a mocking brow.

"Thanks to you." He wrapped a rough hand behind my head and pressed his mouth to mine. His beard chafed my face. His cedar scent surrounded me. His lips found my ear. "You did it." A thrill went through me as he nuzzled my cheek. "The moonstone was not the real power. It was you. The mage needed to possess you, and you wouldn't give yourself to him."

"I had given myself to another," I murmured. I went to my tiptoes to press my brow to his. "Ragnar... thank you for saving me."

"Thank you for saving the world." He threaded his fingers through my hair, and tugged my head back. "Did I not tell you to wait for me?"

"I always break my promises," I whispered against his lips. He slanted his head, kissing me hard.

A slow clap made us turn. "So touching," Loki said.

Ragnar pulled me closer, glaring at Loki. "You are not a man."

"No. I am a god." Loki sketched a bow.

"I knew it," Ragnar muttered. "I would have won that contest."

My laugh broke out of me, loud enough to rouse birds from their trees. The branches overhead parted, and light streamed down upon the three of us, as if the whole day wanted to rejoice with me. Power moved inside me, threatening to overflow. My heart strained.

"You have some things to learn," Loki told me. He settled a hand on me and my insides eased. "Do not worry, I will teach you."

Ragnar shook his head at Loki. "What did you do?"

"She was dying. It was the best way," Loki defended himself. "And now she has what she always wanted. Right, Rosalind?"

"Right," I said, still uncertain. Loki had awoken my power. Was I truly a goddess? "What now?"

"Up to you, really. The battle's over. The quest is done," Loki said. "Everyone's returning to Berserker mountain. To celebrate with a feast and fuck like bunnies in their lodges, and, I assume, live happily ever after. Boring!" He patted his mouth, faking a yawn.

"Do you want to return?" Ragnar asked me.

I bit my lip.

"Or..." Loki held up a finger. "I can teach you how to handle your powers. We could travel the nine worlds together. There are so many adventures to have. Myself, I prefer not to remain in one place too long." He cocked his head to the side. "What say you, Rosalind? Will you join me?"

I heaved a breath, and turned to Ragnar. "What about you? Do you wish to go home?"

"You are my home," he replied.

I closed my eyes a moment, then faced Loki again, and nodded.

"Let us be off then," Loki said. "But first... a quick peek at the celebration. The Berserkers have gathered on their mountain. The spaewives are safe in their lodges with their children at their sides. They will find happiness." He waved a hand, and a smaller portal appeared in the mists.

I saw a young woman, her features similar to my sister Aspen's, with the same white-blonde hair. It *was* Aspen, older, grown into a woman, with a spray of freckles across her nose. She was healthy, laughing, waving to two warriors behind her.

My breath caught. This was a vision of the future.

"We can return to visit her, often," Loki offered.

I nodded. "I'd like that. But first... a few adventures?"

"Yes." Loki rubbed his hands together. Magic flared, and I felt my own power surge in answer. Everything about my life was new, and strange, but it was no matter. I was alive, and Ragnar, Loki and I were together.

A portal appeared before us. Beyond it was a forest much like this one, with mist drifting between the tall trees.

"Fate has granted us a long, long life. Now, we have only to go live it." With a trickster's grin, Loki held out his hand. I reached behind me and grasped Ragnar's, then took Loki's, and the three of us marched forward, onto a new page of our story.

* * *

THANK you for reading the Berserker series! I intend to write more books as my muse directs. Download the Berserker freebie and stay on my newsletter to be in the know about what's next for the brides on Berserker Mountain.

THANK you again for supporting the series.

LOVE,
Lee

FREE BOOK

Get a secret Berserker book, Bred by the Berserkers (only to the awesomesauce fans on Lee's email list)
Click here to get started…https://geni.us/BredBerserker

WANT MORE BERSERKERS?

These fierce warriors will stop at nothing to claim their mates…

The Berserker Saga

<u>Sold to the Berserkers</u> - – Brenna, Samuel & Daegan
<u>Mated to the Berserkers</u> - – Brenna, Samuel & Daegan
<u>Bred by the Berserkers (FREE novella only available at www.leesavino.com)</u> - – Brenna, Samuel & Daegan
<u>Taken by the Berserkers</u> – Sabine, Ragnvald & Maddox
<u>Given to the Berserkers</u> – Muriel and her mates
Claimed by the Berserkers – Fleur and her mates

Berserker Brides

Rescued by the Berserker – Hazel & Knut
Captured by the Berserkers – Willow, Leif & Brokk
Kidnapped by the Berserkers – Sage, Thorbjorn & Rolf
Bonded to the Berserkers – Laurel, Haakon & Ulf

Berserker Babies – the sisters Brenna, Sabine, Muriel, Fleur
and their mates
Night of the Berserkers – the witch Yseult's story
Owned by the Berserkers – Fern, Dagg & Svein
Tamed by the Berserkers — Sorrel, Thorsteinn & Vik

Mastered by the Berserkers — Juliet, Jarl & Fenrir

Berserker Warriors

Ægir *(formerly titled The Sea Wolf)*
Siebold

ALSO BY LEE SAVINO

Contemporary Romance

Royal Bad Boy

I'm not falling in love with my arrogant, annoying, sex god boss.
Nope. No way.

Royally Fake Fiancé

The Duke of New Arcadia has an image problem only a fiancé can fix.
And I'm the lucky lady he's chosen to play Cinderella.

Beauty & The Lumberjacks

After this logging season, I'm giving up sex. For...reasons.

Her Marine Daddy

My hot Marine hero wants me to call him daddy...

Her Dueling Daddies

Two daddies are better than one.

Innocence: dark mafia romance with Stasia Black

I'm the king of the criminal underworld. I always get what I want. And she
is my obsession.

Beauty's Beast: a dark romance with Stasia Black

Years ago, Daphne's father stole from me. Now it's time for her to pay her
family's debt...with her body.

Paranormal romance

The Berserker Saga and Berserker Brides (menage werewolves)

These fierce warriors will stop at nothing to claim their mates.

Draekons (Dragons in Exile) with Lili Zander (menage alien dragons)

Crashed spaceship. Prison planet. Two big, hulking, bronzed aliens who turn into dragons. The best part? The dragons insist I'm their mate.

Bad Boy Alphas with Renee Rose (bad boy werewolves)

Never ever date a werewolf.

ABOUT LEE SAVINO

Lee Savino is a USA today bestselling author of smexy romance. Smexy, as in "smart and sexy." Find her in the Goddess Group on facebook and download a free book at www.leesavino.com!

If you want more menage, check out the Draekon series. If you want more sexy werewolves, check out my Alpha series. Lee has more books but those two series should hold you for awhile. ;)

Find her at:
www.leesavino.com